BLOODSUCKER CITY

A Novella

JIM TOWNS

CASTLE BRIDGE MEDIA
DENVER, COLORADO, USA

CASTLE BRIDGE MEDIA
Denver, Colorado
Edited by Jason Henderson
Edited & Designed by In Churl Yo
Cover by In Churl Yo
Cover Illustration by Jim Towns
Cover photos by Clement Falize/Unsplash, Clement Souchet/Unsplash,
Ganapathy Kumar/Unsplash, Larry Farr/Unsplash

PRELUDE

WHEN THE FIENDS FIRST SLITHERED onto the shores of our continent long ago—spat up by the sea like something rotten it could not digest—they did not at all look as they did later.

For even as all natural things grow and change and evolve, so too do all things unnatural: though not nearly in the same fashion.

1.

7 September, 1933

TALL BUILDINGS WITH BLACKENED WINDOWS rose up on either side of Lena as she walked home from work. The noises of the city sounded all about her—loud in her ears, and yet distant: trains pulling out of the warehouse district, the horns of taxi cabs over on Belle Avenue. The harsh clarion of a police siren somewhere many blocks away rose up—and then just as quickly faded away. And above everything, the blind eyes of windows stared down.

Lena hurried along, anxious to get home to her son Jonathan. She stared at the ground as she walked. She was lovely and pale, a petite young woman with fire-red hair tied tightly back, wearing a long coat over her flimsy cocktail waitress outfit.

If I'm lucky he'll already have put himself to bed, she thought. Then she could have a quiet moment to herself, maybe even read a page or two from her digest, before putting out the light and crawling into the small bed beside him. She would let her eyes close while listening to his gentle breathing, and in a moment she'd be asleep, too.

Theirs wasn't what anyone would have called a good situation, but it was the best one Lena could manage. Once Freddie wasn't around anymore, it had been all she could do to get out of bed for a while. His death benefit didn't last long, and very soon the bills had begun to pile up again. She'd had

4

to go back to the nightclub and beg for her old job back. She could remember sitting in the hard chair in Lonnie's shabby back office, staring up at his grizzled face. His hand had reached out and stroked her chin. His smile had had no warmth in it.

Lena hustled past several young hooligans who were smoking and leaning against a bar frontage. She could feel them leering at her as she hurried along, and pulled the collar of her coat tighter around her, checking its bottom hem. After Freddie, she'd thought of finding a new man—someone to help provide for her and her boy. She'd had a few suitors make her offers. But her married life had been brutal, and she worried about getting caught up in something too quickly, so Lena had abstained. It was better this way. Hard, but better.

She took the three flights of rickety steps up to their apartment slowly, opened the door, entered and closed it once more, locking its assorted deadbolts, chains and latches. Hopefully sometime soon they'd be able to get out of this rat trap. *Maybe I should try to get a job downtown*, she thought. After all she'd always done well in school, and been able to pick up new things quickly.

She saw the light over the small dining table was still on. Jonathan had likely left it burning, wasting electricity. Removing her coat, she made an effort to shake the damp out of it before hanging it up.

"Jonathan? Jonathan, I hope you're ready for bed, it's almost ten..."

Lena took a few steps into the hallway and froze, as her brain struggled to make sense what she was seeing:

A small contorted body, lying in the center of the floor. Her legs quickly began to fail, and she held onto the doorway for support as she sank to the ground.

"No... no, no. No, no...."

She could see Jonathan staring at her with clouded, dim eyes. His cheek rested on the dark wood floor, and his arms and legs were bent at uncomfortable angles. He made little tiny rapid breaths, which wheezed out of the gaping tear in his throat. A very small pool of blood had collected on the floor beneath the wound.

Her lower limbs useless, Lena began to drag herself forward towards her boy.

"Jonathan... Jonathan, no... no, no..."

It seemed to take minutes, but she finally reached him, taking his face in her hands, gently brushing his lank hair back from his face, and ever-so-gently picking up his head to rest on her lap. Her mind was a blank. A screen had fallen over her vision and she couldn't think past the horror that was in front of her.

"No, honey... no, no... no no....."

Jonathan's hazy blue eyes rolled up to look at her with a confused expression, as if he was seeing her from very far away and it required much effort to make out her form.

"Honey? Honey, it's me. It's mama." Her tears fell onto his forehead as she cradled his small, shaking body. And then gradually the already dim light faded out of those eyes altogether, and he was gone.

Lena struggled to breathe. She had to fight to get enough air in her lungs to scream.

"No...no...no, baby, no, no NO! NOOOOOO!!!!!"

As she wailed, the door behind her was kicked in and several policemen entered, but she didn't hear it. The officers froze a moment at the sight before them, but she didn't notice. They slowly approached her, their revolvers raised—but Lena didn't see them. And she didn't feel them when they grabbed her under her shoulders. She only came to when they began pulling her away from her boy's body. Then she cried out, swiping their arms away, screaming, fighting to hold on to her son. But there were too many of them, and finally they pulled her free, and dragged her out of the apartment. Lena clutched at the doorjamb, struggling to keep his her son's body in sight, even as the others knelt over him.

"NO! No you leave him alone! You don't bother him!" She heard her own voice wail as if it were someone else's. A crazy woman, driven mad in a moment by unknowable grief.

She kept staring at Jonathan 's body until she was pulled away from the door and down the steps, and a gathering darkness grew around her, numbing her limbs, quieting her voice, then finally overtaking her in a deep well of black until she knew no more.

2.

LENA HAD BEEN STRIPPED TO her undergarments and sat in a bare room handcuffed to a plain, splintery chair. The side of her face was swollen and cut, and blood dripped from her nose and mouth. That had happened in the squad car on the way to the station. Or maybe it had happened in her apartment? A red fog had crept into the periphery of her vision, and she had difficulty remembering anything clearly now. Everything surrounding her seemed foreign and remote: not quite tangible and certainly not important. All that was important was to hold on to the memory: her last memory of his face. Jonathan's face, lying so very still on the old rug. Eyes closed. At peace. She had to hold on to it with everything she could.

A jarring blow struck the side of her skull, making her head snap painfully sideways on her neck. A voice shouted something very close to her, but she couldn't understand it and anyway she didn't want to—she just wanted to remember.

Another blow, this time to the other side of her head. Words began to seep in through the veil, and as they penetrated to her mind she looked up to see a large man in shirtsleeves standing over her. The overhead bulb cast a bleary halo around his balding head, and his voice slowly crept into her awareness.

"Why did you kill your son?"

Her own voice sounded weak and brittle to her ears: "I didn't... I wouldn't..."

She got slugged again for that.

"Then how about you tell us who did?"

"I have no idea..."

Another voice came from somewhere behind her.

"Ya'll gonna have to do a whole helluva lot better than that, girlie."

She was suddenly aware of the dryness of her throat. Some water would—

"Please—"

The shirtsleeve man's fist slammed into her stomach, knocking the breath out of her and folding her over. She gasped and could see blood drooling into her lap from her mouth. Anger grew inside her.

"Stop it!"

"Stop what? Stop asking you why you killed your boy?"

"I didn't kill my boy. I found him... I found him and he was—"

Her voice went away of its own accord. The memory. Her boy. Jonathan. For an instant she'd forgotten his face. She couldn't do that. They'd taken everything from her: her coat, her shoes, her work clothes, her purse. The little photo of Jonathan in the folding frame she kept close at all times.

As she tried to straighten up, something else caught her eye, penetrating through the red fog. A vague figure: lurking in the darkness well beyond the light's pale glow. A very still shadow that seemed somehow darker than the black surrounding it.

She was cuffed upside the head again. Her hair was grabbed, pulling her face up into the light. A harsh voice whispered in her ear:

"We're not gonna let you get away with this, you know... you're gonna pay for what you did."

"I didn't do anything..." Lena gasped. "He was like that when I—"

She was hit in the cheek again, snapping her head around.

"Honey, this is gonna keep going until you stop lying and start telling us the truth."

"I'm not—I'm telling the truth!"

She was hit again.

8

"Please, stop... I can't..."

"Can't what?"

"Can't face the facts of what you did tonight?"

"Your son is dead."

His face flickered before her.

"I know."

"Just a boy. A little boy. What could he possibly have done to make you so angry?"

"He didn't do anything!"

"Then why did you kill him?"

"I DON'T KNOW!"

The shouting voices abruptly stopped. As one, the men backed away from her, falling away into the shadows beyond the glow of the light. Lena's breath caught in her throat at the realization of what she'd just said.

"No, please... I—I didn't hurt him... Please, I can't think straight..."

But the shirtsleeve man was gone now. They were all faded away, only the too-still figure remained, watching.

"No, wait, please! I didn't mean it! To say— I didn't mean to say..." her voice broke: "Please..."

Her head fell and she sagged in the chair.

•   •   •

The Judge's gavel slammed down, startling her. She'd gone away again, lost in memory. But now she was brought forcibly back to consciousness.

The courtroom was old and stiflingly hot. Lena stood in the docks facing the bench. Her wrists and ankles were still handcuffed. Her face was still bruised, and her hair hung limp. She wasn't sure how much time had passed since she'd found Jonathan. Hours. Maybe days? She couldn't remember how long the trial itself had been going on for, but it didn't feel like it had been very long at all.

The judge banged his gavel again.

"Elena Fitzgerald Cole, based on your own admission during questioning, as well as the overwhelming circumstantial evidence of your culpability, you have been found guilty by this court of the cold-blooded murder of your own son. Taking into account the heinousness of your crime, and the callous cruelty by which you let him bleed to death, while showing no remorse whatsoever, I have no choice but to sentence you to life in prison without the possibility of parole, to be served at Steelegate Prison for Women. Sentence is to be carried out immediately. And may God have mercy on your poor, depraved soul."

The final blow of the judge's gavel came, and decayed slowly away in her ears, lingering it seemed for a long time.

Strong hands led Lena away.

3.

THE LONG ROAD TO STEELGATE was unpaved and rutted, and the rear of the paddy wagon bounced crazily on rusted steel springs as it slogged its slow way towards the prison.

Lena sat numbly with her hands and ankles shackled to a hard bench seat. She was the only prisoner in the back of the vehicle, and a young guard sat opposite her: his shotgun ready. He'd been staring at her from the moment she'd climbed inside, but they'd been going for a half hour before she finally looked up and met his gaze.

"Go on. Say what you're thinking."

The young man blinked. He was sallow-complexioned with pockmarked cheeks, and fit poorly into his woolen police coat.

"What kinda mother kills her own child?"

Lena stared at him a while before answering.

"No kind of mother, I guess."

The two settled back into grim silence. The ride became momentarily smoother as the lorry rumbled over a cement bridge, which crossed a narrow but turbulent creek.

The guard nodded out the barred window: "You wanna take a look at your new home? You know, seeing as how it's the last time you're gonna see it from the outside."

Lena glanced up through the narrow opening, and her eyes widened.

A few miles down the road she could see a tall cliff face, which rose up abruptly from the surrounding marsh, as if it was the pinnacle end of some great and forgotten mountain chain. The rocky wall climbed up and up, curving outward into space as it did, and at its crest a man-made structure seemed to grow out of the stone, rising tall and narrow against the sky like some medieval keep. In fact it was so welded into its base, it was hard to note for certain at what point the natural rock ended, and the masonry of the building began.

"That's it, huh?"

He nodded. "That's it. Steelegate. Only the worst of the worst end up here. Nobody, and I mean nobody, gets out."

"Never?"

"Place was built as a prison for Yankees during the war. Not one of 'em ever got free, not even after the war ended. So you best put that out of your mind right now."

The wagon gave a harsh lurch, and she could feel the front end tilt up as they started to climb.

"Cutback Road. Only way up or down to the prison gate."

To keep from sliding, Lena held tightly to the chain that held her fixed to the bench, and even so the sharp metal of her leg shackles dug painfully into the bones of her ankles. But she refused to let herself show any discomfort. For a little bit she went away to her safe place, where Jonathan was still waiting for her in their tiny apartment. She was on her way home, and after dinner they'd play cards at the table before bedtime. She'd been teaching him to play gin rummy, but he'd often get the spades and clubs mixed up.

Another jolt knocked her back to the present, and the pain in her ankles returned. They climbed in this sluggish fashion for at least another half-hour, though it was hard for Lena to judge. As they began, she could see glimpses of tall brush and leafy trees passing by on either side of the road. These eventually gave way to clumps of tall pines, and soon there was only the sporadic tree, bent and twisted and clinging to the rough rocky ground. Finally there were only giant piles of boulders, many of them sharply squared off where they'd been quarried for construction of the prison. Obviously that had been a long time ago, because those chiseled edges were now eroded and rounded with the years and sun and weather.

Night had fully fallen by the time they were approaching Steelgate's exterior wall. Lena could see several brilliant spotlights on either side of the road that shone upward, slashing blazing yellow arcs across thousands and thousands of tightly interlacing bricks that formed the prison's outer curtain.

At the guard gate the vehicle finally stopped, its engine stalling into a sputtering silence. The wagon's rear doors were opened and two prison guards stared in at her, playing a harsh flashlight on her face.

"What we got?"

Her guard's voice cracked just a little bit when he answered them: "Child killer. Life sentence. Here's her orders:" he handed them a clipboard.

One of the guards took her sheet, shining his torch on it. They wore similar suits of dark grey, with double-breasted tunics and straight trousers and funny looking squat brimmed caps. Each wore a thick leather belt from which a heavy wooden billy club dangled.

One of the guards caught her staring: "Tha's right, young lady:- thisee here—" he tickled the cudgel with calloused digits: "—this is my friend Betsy... see first I talk, and then if ya'll don't listen, Betsy here starts doing the talkin.' He grinned. It was obvious to her that he enjoyed giving this speech: "Trust me, ya'll don't wanna hear what Betsy has to say."

"How 'bout we put a pipe in it for now, Clayton, that be all right?" the other guard admonished him. This one was older, taller and mustached—a man used to being in charge. He stepped up onto the back of the wagon, leaving the doors open.

"It's okay, I'll ride 'em in. Hey Les, open her up!"

At his order Lena heard a great groan of metal as heavy bolts were released and something large creaked open on great hinges. The lorry puttered to life again and trundled its way through the gate and into the courtyard. Past where the older guard hung on, she saw one half of a mighty iron door close behind her, even as a second chain fence closed after it. This one was strung through with barbed wire: she could see the little flowers of jagged steel catching the light.

A jarring stop and the wagon guard, after passing his shotgun to the other, pulled a ring of keys off his belt, reached down and unlocked the padlock holding Lena's chains in place. He nodded her out the door without another word, and she took two cautious steps to the back gate of the truck, only to have the prison guard roughly grab her around her upper arm and yank her out of the truck with such force she almost landed on her head.

"Just you stay put right there, missy." He handed the truck guard back his rifle, and Lena felt her arms jerked behind her back and a new set of manacles now clapped painfully around her wrists.

Her thin dress did nothing to keep out the night's chill, and Lena stood there shivering as she looked around. The outer courtyard of the prison was an unusual triangle shape. Two sheer walls rose up on either side without window or door, angled towards each other so they met on either side of the great gate. A wooden barn took up most of the space to her left and seemed to function as both a garage for autos as well as a maintenance shed; and a raised wooden walkway ran along the wall on the other side, probably for loading and unloading larger trucks.

"Okay turn around now."

Turning, Lena saw the third wall was the true façade of Steelgate—an imposing keep that soared even taller than the other two. It seemed to narrow as it went up, but that might have been a trick of the eye from her lowly perspective. Lena had never seen anything this large in her entire life. She'd never even seen a picture of anything built on this scale, and her mind tried to grasp how something this huge could have been built this far away from anything—the manpower and materials required must have been enormous.

Her thoughts were cut short as she once more felt the meaty hand of the mustached guard grasp her arm in a pincer-like grip.

"This way. Step lively, missy."

She was led up a short flight of wide stone steps to a tall wooden door, banded and bolted with rusted red iron. The heavy door seemed to swing onerously open of its own power, and Lena could just make out a long tunnel-like passage beyond, lit occasionally with dim flickering bulbs. Then she was through the door and listening to it clanging shut behind her. Steelgate had swallowed her up.

4.

THE LIGHT SHINING ON HER was blinding, rendering the entire world into either a white hot glare, or else a hazy shadow. Lena stood stripped naked in the tile room—every stitch of clothing had been yanked off her. She could hear the male voices of the guards laughing and making inaudible (-but unmistakably crude) -comments from somewhere behind the light.

Then, without warning, she felt freezing cold water smash into her bare body and she was slammed against the cold tile wall by the terrifying pressure of a fire hose. The icy blast cut right through her, making it feel like a hundred million tiny needles stabbing her skin. Orders were shouted at her: to raise her arms above her head, to turn her palms outward, to turn around, to lift her feet and show her soles to the guards; to bend over—at which point she received such a painful blast from the hose between her legs that she lost her footing and collapsed headfirst, gasping as water blasted up her nose and filled her mouth, choking her.

Finally, mercifully, it stopped.

The laughing, however, continued.

•　　•　　•

Twenty minutes later she stood, still naked, in the prison's clinic. She'd been led there holding a stack of bedding and clothing by the guards, without having been allowed to dress. They'd marched her down a great long vast hallway, past rows and rows of barred darkened cells, and from them she'd heard women's voices calling out at her, casting insults and slurs—some cursing her, some cursing the guards, some just cursing. But every time she'd begun to turn her eyes left or right, she was rewarded with the end of a billy club thrust in the small of her bare back. So she had walked, her crimson hair lank and dripping, water running down over her exposed breasts and stomach, leaving small bare footprints behind her. It was humiliating. It physically hurt. But still Lena refused to let herself cry. She wouldn't give them the satisfaction. She struggled to make her mind take her away from it all, but her place of contentment seemed further away now, and more difficult to reach.

The clinic was a series of three rooms that ran off one another in an L shape, as poorly lit as everything else she'd seen so far at Steelgate, but at least slightly more comfortable. There was a wooden desk and chairs in the center with a lamp and several notebooks and ledgers, a row of filing cabinets, glass specimen cases, and an examination table with stirrups. She stood shivering next to it as a female doctor performed her examination.

The doctor was middle-aged. She was tall and narrow and had an angular but attractive and not-altogether unkindly face, Lena thought. A white coat covered much of her somewhat-faded paisley dress. She wore her colorless hair pulled tightly back, and a delicate pair of gold-framed spectacles perched on her nose. The plaque on her desk read *Dr. Johanna Mears, MD.*

Doctor Mears had a manila folder open and was scribbling notes onto forms inside it as she asked Lena questions.

"Says here twenty-nine."

"That's right. Can I get dressed now?"

That got her a look over the glasses: "You can get dressed when I say you can get dressed," She checked her notes. "This is your first time incarcerated?"

"Yes."

"But you have a history of violence? Troubled childhood? Foster care?

16

Reform school?"

"No."

"Hmm." The doctor made a note.

"Any other type of aberrant physical behavior?"

"Such as?"

"Fainting spells, blackouts, lost time, seizures?"

"No. Nothing like that."

She made more notes.

"Very well. Please bend over."

Lena complied.

"No history of venereal disease?"

"No."

"Okay, you can stand up. Hemophilia?"

Lena paused: "What?"

"Excessive bleeding. Poor coagulant count in the blood."

"No, I—I don't think so."

Dr. Mears scribbled more notes.

"Just the one child, then?"

Lena hadn't been prepared for that question. It came out of nowhere. Unbeckoned, the image of Jonathan flashed before eyes for a millisecond.

Lena tried, but she couldn't make herself answer the doctor's question right away. She was too focused on fighting the tears that suddenly wanted to cascade from her eyes. She was winning, but she couldn't keep her lip from trembling just a bit.

The doctor looked up when she didn't answer: "Just the one child?"

Lena could just manage a whisper.

"Yes. Just the one."

"Fine. You can get dressed now."

•　　•　　•

It was almost totally dark in the Wardens' main office. The room wasn't overly wide but it was long, and between that and its tall barrel vaulted ceiling, it could almost have felt like the naive of a church, only it didn't in the slightest.

At the far end from the entrance was a great leaded window which ran from floor to roof, and which provided a wide vista of the prison's courtyard below, the walls surrounding it, and beyond those the great flat plains stretching out for miles into the distance. Tonight it also revealed a vast bank of heavy cumulous clouds rolling in fast from the west, their roiling underbellies dark against the weak light of a rising crescent moon.

A tall slender figure stood in front of the window, watching the turbulent sky with fascination until, on the far side of the room, the door opened. A swath of light from the hallway swept across the floor at its opening, illuminating first a long wine-colored rug, then a tall wooden table surrounded by a collection of high backed chairs, before finally reaching the figure and running up long legs and a tall, narrow torso, to stop just at its neck. The figure was male, wearing a tightly tailored suit with a high collar and a string-like, antiquated necktie. The limbs seemed almost of disproportionate length, and this included the fingers of the pallid hands, which were elongated and narrow.

The guard at the door was the mustached one who'd escorted Lena into the prison. Alone with the figure, the big man stood uneasily, shifting his weight from one foot to the other.

"Just wanted to let you know, Warden Skelly, the wagon came in and brought that new girl—the one that killed her kid."

Warden Skelly's voice was soft and deep: "Excellent, Bruno. We'll give her the day to get situated, and then let's meet her tomorrow evening."

Bruno nodded, "Yes, sir."

"That will be all, Bruno. Thank you."

"Yes sir."

The door closed, leaving the Head Warden, once more, in darkness.

•   •   •

Two guards led Lena down the hallway of the cellblock. She now wore her prison outfit, and carried a towel with a few toiletries and a bar of strong-smelling soap. The outfit was little more than a plain, sacklike linen dress of dull white, the ratty hem of which grazed her knees; and a pair of slipper-like shoes with thin soles, also a dull white, which were a half-size too big for her.

"Alright, here you are." The guards stopped and turned, and Lena saw her cell: A narrow room maybe six feet wide with a steel door that only had a single, small barred window in it. One of the guards opened the door with a squeak and a clang. It was dark inside the cell.

"Welcome to your new digs, honey."

Lena stared at it. She couldn't make her feet move, so the other guard gave her an ungentle prod with his nightstick.

"Go on, then. We don't got all night."

She stumbled in, and the guards closed the door behind her with a shrill metallic *clank*, turning the key.

"Wardens'll meet with you tomorrow. Don't let the bedbugs bite!"

The two laughed as they walked away, their echoing footsteps finally dying out. Silence fell. Lena stared around the dark room, waiting for her eyes to adjust. A narrow shaft of light came in through a high narrow window in the rear wall, slashing across the featureless cinderblock walls, the hard floor, crude toilet, and bunk beds. Then a shadow shifted on the lower bed, and Lena could see that someone was sitting there. She took a nervous step back.

"Save it, sister. You don't have to worry about me, at least."

The other woman slowly rose, and took a step towards her. She was perhaps a few years older than Lena, but it was hard to tell. She was dark-complexioned, taller than Lena; with a shock of black hair, thin lips and deep set, haunted eyes.

"My name's Yvonne. So you're her, huh?"

"Her who?" Lena knew enough to understand it was vital for her to stand her ground in this moment.

"The baby killer. We heard you were coming in tonight."

She stared at the taller woman. "I didn't kill anybody."

Yvonne stared back into her eyes for a long moment, then shrugged: "'Course you didn't." It was hard to tell if she believed Lena in the slightest, or not.

Yvonne backed off a step in the cramped space: "Okay, then: looks like

we're gonna be bunkies... for a while, at least. I'll give you the nickel tour."
She pointed to each object as she listed them: "Bed, pisser, and there's a little
shelf there you can put your stuff. The other one's mine and you don't go
anywhere near it, understand?"

"Sure."

"Guess that's about it, except I got the lower bunk. Seniority rules
'round here."

Lena nodded. "That's fine."

"You don't snore or piss the bed, do ya?"

"Not that I've been told."

"Good, you and me should get along fine. Now I'm going back to sleep,
if that's okay with you."

"Sure. I mean, of course. I'll be quiet."

Her cellmate lay back down on the lower bunk. "That would be much
appreciated."

Lena gently put her little pile of things on her shelf, took off her shoes
and with some effort in the dark, managed to climb up to her narrow bed.

"Best thing's to keep close to the wall, so if you roll over you don't
fall out."

"Right... thanks." Lena pulled the scratchy blanket over herself, laying
her head on a thin, musty smelling pillow. She stared out the small window at
the night sky beyond for a few moments. It felt like just moments ago she'd
been home in her own place, with her boy. Her new roommate's voice drifted
up from below.

"They rough on you? Cops and guards and doctors and such?"

"Some, yeah."

A pause. "How old was your kid?"

"Eleven."

"They're nice at that age... still just a little bit innocent."

"Yeah. Hey, um..."

"Yvonne."

"Yvonne. Thanks. You're the first person in a while that's been—"

"Don't get all choked up about it. And don't get too used to this cell,
or me, or anything for that matter. Stuff's got a way of changing real quick

20

around here."

"Okay."

They lay there for a bit in silence.

"I thought... I thought there'd be more noise."

"Not at night. Daytime this place can be a madhouse, but at night—well, it's best to keep quiet." There was a moment's pause and Lena could hear springs squeak as Yvonne shifted around below her. "Now if it's alright with you I'm gonna get me some shuteye. Lord knows, I need all the beauty rest I can get."

Lena smiled just a bit at that, still staring out at the night sky beyond the window until her eyes finally closed.

•   •   •

She was cradling her son's limp body in her arms, screaming... screaming. Hands were tearing her away. She fought them, but there were too many, and they were too strong. She was losing her grip on him. He was going away. She couldn't see him clearly anymore through a wall of black and blue wool, past the shiny brass buttons and sharp-pointed badges.

Lena shot up in bed, covered in sweat, breathing rapidly. As sleep fled and awareness came back to reveal where she was, she became aware of an eerie feeling, like she was being watched.

Through the small barred window, a shadow blocked the light from the prison block hallway. The shadow had twin points of glittering light: tiny unwinking specks that bore into her like razors. Lena felt an acute pang of loss and grief flash through her, and then dissipate. She blinked, rubbing the last of the sleep from her eyes.

The shadow and its glittering specks were gone.

Slowly she lay back down, pulling her threadbare covers back over her. Her eyes lingered on the door where she was certain she'd seen the shadow. She started a bit when Yvonne whispered from below:

"Looks like they got their eyes on you..."

5.

12 September

THE NEXT MORNING LENA WOKE to find Yvonne already up and out of her bunk. A shrill buzzer rang, startling her.

"Breakfast."

She dressed hurriedly, and when the guard unlocked their cell door she followed Yvonne down the long walkway to the end of their cellblock. The barred gate there was open this morning, and the two fell into a long line with female prisoners from their cell block and others, perhaps two hundred in all: each wearing the same linen sack dress, the same flat shoes. As a group, the prisoners all made their way into the Commissary.

It was a vast room with ceiling lights high overhead, each one protected by a wire mesh grill. Some kind of stage had been constructed a few feet off the floor at the end of the room, and next to it was the food counter. A group of women prisoners wearing aprons over their sack dresses served out a sloppy mess of runny colorless eggs, hard plain slices of toast and lukewarm coffee. Lena took her tray and followed Yvonne to a seat near the far side of the room.

Her cellmate stared at her as she sat down.

"Okay, girlie, it's your first day and everything's all new to you. I get it. But you're not my understudy. At some point you're gonna have to stop tracing my footsteps. Find your own place to sit and all. We clear?"

Lena nodded that she understood, and began eating. Her stomach was empty—she hadn't had any supper the previous night—but even as hungry as she was, the food was vaguely repulsive. The toast tasted of metal and the eggs had a sour flavor, like they had been cooked in dirty pans or mixed with stagnant water.

"Is it always—?"

"This bad? Pretty much. Except for Thursdays."

"What's Thursdays?"

"Meat Loaf. I don't know why, but it's pretty good."

Lena went back to trying to get her food down. She glanced around the room, getting her first good look at her fellow inmates. All were adult women, and most of them were in their twenties or thirties, with very few older females present, Lena noticed. She had expected to be confronted by aggressive types. Based solely on what she'd seen at the pictures, Lena had expected fights and other rows, and a menagerie of angry and dangerous women. The women of Steelgate, however, seemed mostly sad. Sad in a deep, abiding way that transcended mere angst or sorrow. Her mind told her that maybe they were all filled with regret from the deeds that had led them here, but then she reflected on her own case. She was an innocent woman, and here she was. Lena wondered how many other women she was seeing were here on false charges as well. A few? Half? There was no way to know.

Her meandering gaze fell on a tall figure in a black suit, standing in the shadows near the curtains of the stage risers. His features were difficult to make out: he stood tall and erect, all in black, with his fingers clasped before him. His eyes seemed to catch and reflect the light of the room in an uncanny way.

Lena nodded to Yvonne: "Who's that?"

Yvonne looked over without fully looking, a talent she'd obviously developed from much practice here.

"That's one of them."

"One of who?"

"The Wardens." Yvonne put her fork down. "They keep their distance for the most part, leave the discipline and such to the guards."

"He looks... I've never seen—"

"You won't anywhere else. Someone told me once that they've been running this place since before the Great War, and even before that."

"They live here? With us?"

Yvonne nodded: "Up in the tower. You saw it coming in. That's the Administration Building. They mostly stay there during the day, doing— administrative stuff."

"But?"

"But at night they like to prowl about, keeping an eye on things."

As Lena looked over she could have sworn the Warden turned his uncanny gaze to stare straight at her. She quickly looked down at her tray. In the half-second they'd locked eyes, a turgid unease had washed through the pit of her belly, and she was reminded of the glittering eyes from the night before.

"I think he saw me staring."

"It's fine, you'll be meeting them soon enough. For your admission interview. It's a standard thing. State required or something like that. Do yourself a favor when you go. Answer their questions. Be polite. Be submissive."

"Okay."

Yvonne leaned in.

"DON'T claim to be innocent. They don't want to hear it. And it's not worth making them angry. Trust me, you don't want to make them angry."

Lena went back to eating. When they were told to stand up and file out at the end of the meal, she noticed the spot where she'd seen the Warden was empty.

•　　•　　•

It was a few hours later, and the guards had led most of the women out into an open space with high walls, which she'd heard the others call simply the Yard. Yvonne had been pulled onto a cleaning detail, so Lena had walked the large circle with the others for a bit, and now was sitting alone on a bench by the great stone wall of the Administration Building, watching the other women walking here and there around the yard in their identical garb. They stood around and talked, sometimes smoking cigarettes or sometimes, she noticed, just staring off at nothing.

Her view was suddenly blocked when a group of three women stopped in front of her, blocking the sun. Lena squinted up at them.

The closest one was a tall, lean black woman with tightly pulled-back hair, wearing glasses. The second was also tall, with dark blonde hair and an angry look. The third was even taller than the first two, and was also very rotund. Her skin was splotched with red, and Lena could see many of the blood vessels in her nose and cheeks were burst, tracing little purple lines under her skin.

The dark-skinned one glanced to her second: "Newbie?"

The one with short hair nodded.

"Yeah. They brought her in last night."

Lena squinted up at the three: "I'm Lena."

"I don't care what your name is."

"Okay..." Lena looked down. This was more like what she'd been expecting.

The very big girl piped up: "Listen up, sister. There's a way we do things around here. A system."

Lena shook her head. "I'm getting that."

"You think I'm just talking? You cross us, or mess with us, or try to rat us out about *anything*, and I'll personally make sure your stay here gets cut extra short. I'm in for life, it don't matter to me one way or the other."

"Okay."

The dark one spoke again: "Point is, sis, we're all lifers, all of us. Right Greta? Right Hallie?"

The others nodded.

"What I'm saying is, we're all three of us meant to die in here. But I plan on making sure that's a long time from now... a lotta things can happen in that time. Governments have fallen in that time. You get me?"

Lena nodded again. Her knees were quivering, but she worked to not let it show. If she held her temper and kept her wits about her, she hoped to get though this without it turning into a physical altercation. One she'd surely lose, given the odds.

"There's a lot you don't know about how this place works, girl..." the

25

short-haired one called Greta said. "Most likely you won't last long enough to find out, but in the meantime you watch it, okay? Don't go sticking that little button nose of yours anyplace it don't belong."

The three stared down at her for a tense moment.

"So is that it, or..?" Lena surprised herself with her cockiness, and was rewarded by being grabbed by the collar of her ratty garment. The black girl's face was very near hers:

"Think of us like a hospitality committee. You get one visit, and that's it. My name is Helen. You go and try to find someone here who's crossed me. You won't. Because they're not here anymore, get me?"

Lena nodded.

"You just watch your back in here, because nobody else will. Least of all us."

Helen released her, and the trio walked off. As they did, Greta turned to speak over her shoulder, grinning at her:

"Welcome to Bloodsucker City. Enjoy the sun, while it lasts."

Lena watched them go. Only after she was sure they were leaving did she glance up at the bright sun overhead.

•   •   •

The showers.

Lena was in line behind the other women who were waiting their turn, holding their towels and soap. The shower room was large, with hard tile walls and floors. It smelled of damp and chlorine. The line moved slowly: she watched up ahead as the guards would herd six women at a time under the rusted nozzles, watching as they stripped and scrubbed under the water, then barked at them to be done before prodding them out the other side— many of them still struggling to pull on their clothing as they went.

The tall girl standing in line in front of her turned around, and she saw it was Yvonne.

"Long time no see. Made it through your first morning intact?"

Lena shrugged.

"More or less." Even as she spoke, she flinched a bit as Hallie pushed

26

past them, cutting to the front of the line.

"Watch it, comin' through..."

Yvonne shook her head. "In fairness, she needs a shower more than most of us. You meet the hard gang yet?"

"Yeah. In the yard."

Up ahead, they could see Hallie was arguing with another inmate—a petite girl with a short bob Lena had heard called Bonnie—about who was first in line.

"One on three with the hard gang and here you are still in one piece? You may be tougher than you look... which wouldn't be saying much."

The argument ahead had turned into a scuffle. Hallie had grabbed Bonnie in a headlock, and was swinging her around. The other girls were stepping back out of the way of the fracas.

"Hey, leave her alone, Big Hal." Yvonne shouted.

"You mind your beeswax!" the big girl continued to wrestle poor Bonnie into submission.

Yvonne stared: "That girl's gonna tick off the wrong person one of these days..."

Lena took a step back with the rest, watching the scuffle. "I'm not here to fight with anybody." She mumbled. "I'm not here to take sides or make new friends... I just want to——-"

She was abruptly shoved aside as several guards pushed past them, grabbing the two fighting females. Hallie struggled against their grip, and it took three of them to hold her, even with the one called Clayton pressing his nightstick across her thick neck.

"She started it! She cut in line." Hallie yelled.

Bonnie wailed: "Liar!"

"I told her to wait her turn, and she started swinging! She's cracked, I tell you!"

Clayton turned to several nearby women: "Is that true?"

The women glanced at each other, looked up into Hallie's eyes— and nodded.

"LIARS!" Bonnie's voice broke.

Bruno, the older guard who'd escorted Lena into the prison, came in barking orders now, with a half-dozen guards as backup.

"What the hell is this?" he pointed at Bonnie. "Get that one out of here! Take her down to solitary."

Before their eyes, Bonnie's tough demeanor vanished instantly.

"No! NOOOO! I'm sorry... I am! I won't fight anymore, I swear!"

But she was hauled away by two guards, her heels dragging as she hollered.

"Noooo!!!!! PLEASE!!!!"

Yvonne bent down to pick up their towels and soap they'd dropped.

"You were saying something? About what you want to do?"

Lena stared down at the end of the hallway, where Bonnie was pulled through a steel door by the guards into the darkness beyond. The door shut, and she was gone.

"Disappear. I was gonna say... I just want to disappear."

•　　•　　•

Lena was sitting quietly on her bunk, lost in her memories, until something made her look up—a subtle shift. The late afternoon sun had sunk below the level of her narrow window. The air around her had grown ever so slightly colder. It was close to dusk. She contented herself to sit and watch as the amber sky began to quickly fade to pale cerulean, then a darker azure.

She didn't hear the guard approaching until his voice gave her a start.

"Time to go see the Wardens, newbie."

She nodded, climbing down from her bunk as he opened the cell door.

The guard led Lena down the cellblock, the same way as if they were going to the commissary; but before reaching it the guard pulled her towards a set of steel doors. He knocked, waiting, and then knocked again. A key scraped in the lock on the far aide, and the doors opened. A shorter, stockier guard nodded to them as they passed, then closed and locked the heavy doors behind them.

Lena was escorted down a long hallway. Instead of cinderblocks and steel, the walls here were of painted plaster, and wainscoted in dark paneled wood. Large, faded photos adorned the walls: a row of pictures of Steelgate in various stages of construction as armies of men, mighty steam shovels and oxen teams helped build its cyclopean edifice.

She was led into a central atrium with a ceiling so high it disappeared far above, and a staircase wrapping around it, leading up. This, Lena was certain, was the Keep. She and the guard walked up three floors of carpeted stairs until they reached a dimly lit hallway.

"Turn left." The guard ordered.

They walked together down the hall, which was decorated with old, faded tapestries on either side. Massive weavings that seemed to depict the history of the region: old battles and peace treaties, crop harvesting, and then a new industrial revolution. But their story stopped there. *Perhaps*, she thought to herself, *they'd run out of thread.*

Finally they reached the end of the hallway, and another set of double doors: these ones made of dark wood similar to the paneling below—walnut or hickory, maybe. It seemed to Lena that the guard tensed at the threshold, steeling his courage before rapping twice on the door.

A voice on the other side said '*enter*', the doors opened, and Lena was led into the Warden's Office.

•   •   •

Tonight the seven tall chairs of the table were all occupied. The guard led Lena by the arm to a low seat at the table's near end. She kept her eyes downcast as she sat down, as the guard retreated to stand near the door.

She sat thus for a moment before she heard a soft, deep voice spoke.

"Look up at us, child, it's alright." Lena looked up, and got a good look at the Wardens for the first time:

To a one they were all tall and narrowly-built, with long limbs and slender fingers. Lena could see they were all dressed in similar dark suits, which seemed old and out-of-date. Some looked frayed or seemed to have been repaired at some point. All wore white collared shirts and old-fashioned string bow ties. All sat silently, staring at her with what at a casual glance seemed liked friendly smiles; but if one looked closely were really more like expressions of eerie bemusement.

29

The one in the center—even taller than the rest—spoke in the soft buttery voice she'd heard before:

"Good evening, Miss. My name is Warden Skelly. I'm the Head Warden of Steelgate. To my left you see Warden Oberlun, Warden Smithfield and Warden Tarker. These gentlemen to my right are Wardens Kleig, Evers and Tolfison."

He smiled: "It's alright, we don't expect you to remember all that right away. We'll have plenty of time to get to know one another. Warden Evers, would you kindly read our new guest's file aloud for our edification, please?"

Warden Evers rose, holding a sheet of paper before him. How he could see in the dim light escaped Lena.

"Cole, Elena. Age twenty-nine. Is this you?"

Lena nodded.

"Speak up for us, please, Miss," said Warden Skelly.

"Yes. That's me." She said, louder this time.

"Excellent. Please continue, Warden."

"Born Elena Maria Fitzgerald. Married Frederick David Cole twelve years ago, giving birth to a son, Jonathan, soon after."

Lena could have sworn that the Warden had intentionally stressed her son's name. She was determined to not let her voice break.

"Yes."

Warden Evers turned the paper over: "Mister Cole went missing several years ago. Mrs. Cole contacted the authorities, but apparently no trace of him was found."

She could see Warden Skelly's eyebrows raise a fraction.

"Hmm. Unfortunate."

Evers continued: "Miss Cole was granted an *in absentia* divorce two years ago, although she kept her former husband's surname."

She stammered: "It... it's my son's last name. I wanted us... I wanted our names to be the same."

Skelly nodded. "Interesting. Pray go on."

"Miss Cole was arrested eleven days ago in her domicile, after neighbors complained of screams and sounds of a scuffle. Subject was found with the body of the boy, Jonathan, aged eleven."

"This is all accurate?" Skelly asked.

Lena could only nod. "Yes..." she said quietly, then again louder.

Evers was near the bottom of the page now: "Miss Cole was covered in her son's blood. There was some kind of struggle with the officers who responded to the distress call."

"I-- I couldn't let him go. I..."

The Warden that Skelly had identified as Smithfield raised a finger at her.

"Kindly keep your information pertinent to the report, Miss Cole."

Lena nodded.

"Convicted of manslaughter in the first degree by City Court, sentenced to incarceration without possibility of parole for the remainder of her natural life. Remanded to Steelegate Women's Penitentiary to serve out the term of her sentence."

Skelly nodded. "Which I believe brings us the present circumstances. Thank you, Warden Evers. Masterfully read."

Warden Evers bowed slightly, and sat back down. Warden Skelly looked down the table at Lena now.

"Is there anything you would like to add, Miss Cole?"

She looked up: "Anything..?"

"To your narrative. Some detail it perhaps omitted?"

She looked at them all a moment.

"I'm innocent." She said, flatly.

"I'm sorry. Again?"

Lena set her jaw: "I'm innocent. I did not kill my son. I came home from work, and found him on the floor. He... he—"

The Warden she'd seen in the Commissary, Tolifson, held up his hand.

"Miss Cole, this is not a courtroom. You were found just and duly guilty of the crime in a court of law. The debate over your guilt or innocence is over."

Warden Skelly raised his hand a fraction of an inch, and she saw Warden Tolifson sit back as if he'd been struck.

"Now now... we did ask, after all." The authority the Head Warden commanded over the others was unmistakable.

He leaned forward. The way his eyes sparked in the dim light in the

31

room gave Lena the same unnerving feeling as before, in the Commissary.

"You say you're innocent. What do you think actually happened to your son, Miss Cole?"

She paused, choosing her words with care: "I—I don't know. When I found him, he was... he was almost gone. He tried to whisper something, but... but I couldn't hear."

The tears came. She tried to fight them back, but it was too late now. She was crying shamefully in front of the Wardens.

"And your husband? *Mister* Cole?" Warden Tolfison's sibilant voice spoke up.

She looked up: "I'm sorry?"

"I was asking about the disappearance of your husband."

"I don't... know. One evening he went to work, and—and never came back."

The Head Warden sat back in his tall chair: "A great deal of misfortune surrounds you, doesn't it, Miss Cole?"

Lena wiped at her eyes, sniffling back her grief.

"I suppose."

"Misfortune for those around you, I should say. Those who put their trust in you."

He'd managed to get her angry now. Lena knew it was intentional. She knew he was trying to get a reaction, and she shouldn't give it to him, but they had her at such a disadvantage, and she was having a great deal of difficulty managing her emotions.

"I had nothing to do with my husband disappearing. I don't know what happened to him. Just like I don't know what happened to my—"

Warden Skelly raised his hand.

"I believe I speak for all of us when I say we've heard enough."

Skelly rose, causing the other Wardens to glance at each other. He paced slowly around the table towards Lena, moving with only the slightest whisper.

"This is a sad story that my fellow Wardens and I are only too familiar with, Miss Cole. *I'm the victim. I never had a fair chance. The world is against me. It's all just a grand conspiracy.*"

"I'm not a liar, sir."

Skelly paused. His face split into an eerie grin as his eyes pierced her.

"Well, somebody obviously believes you are, because—" He gestured to the walls around them.

"This is *Steelegate*, Miss Cole. Only the worst women come here to stay with us. Those whom society will not miss, and is, in all likelihood, better off without. Murderers, psychotics, pederasts, degenerates... and child killers like yourself. My fellow Wardens and I strive to create an harmonious climate within these walls, for all our sakes. To that end, we will treat you with civility and respect—and will expect nothing less in return from you. We very much hope that this will be the way of our dealings for the duration of your... stay. But do not mistake us. Here in Steelegate, disrespect is met with swift discipline. Misbehavior is dealt with punishment most severe..."

He took a tiny but intimidating step closer to her: "...and any attempts at escape will bring your residence here to the most sudden of conclusions. Do we make ourselves abundantly clear?"

"Abundantly," she said. It took all of Lena's will to meet the Head Warden's uncanny glittering stare, but she managed to for just a few seconds. It was only a tiny victory, but it was a victory nonetheless.

Skelly turned on his heel, retreating back towards the head of the table.

"I'm very glad to hear it. Thank you for your kind attention. You may return to your cell now, Miss Cole—my fellow Wardens and I have other matters to attend to."

She slowly stood, backing up a step or two until she nearly bumped into the guard, who took her by the arm and escorted her out.

Lena risked one final glance over her shoulder as she was led to the door. The Wardens were all still sitting, watching her with seven pairs of uncanny eyes.

"Pleasure meeting you, Miss Cole," Skelly chimed as she was led out the door.

•　　•　　•

Her heavy cell door opened and the guard jostled Lena inside. She couldn't help but wince, as it slammed shut once again behind her.

Yvonne was sitting on her bunk.

"And yet again she returns intact."

"Do they not, sometimes?"

Her cellmate shrugged: "Depends. What did you think of them?"

"The Wardens? I don't know. Strange, I guess..."

Yvonne stared at her a moment, as if deciding whether to say something, then choosing not to.

"Yeah. Strange."

•　　•　　•

A hundred feet below, in the Hole, Bonnie lay curled up in a ball on the floor in almost total darkness, lost in a fitful sleep—when her eye suddenly snapped open. Though she couldn't see anything, she could hear sounds coming from very close by: a creak, a soft movement, a slight chittering noise.

Her breath came fast and shallow as the sounds grew louder, and closer.

6.

30 October

THE GREAT HEAVY GATE SLOWLY rose to reveal a group of wealthy-looking women waiting impatiently. There might have been a baker's dozen of them, and they were all dressed in the finest contemporary *haute couture*: wide-brimmed hats, dresses with rows of huge buttons or wide belts, and calf leather handbags. Some of the ladies were younger. Most were middle-aged or older, and many were on the plump side. The chrome adornments on their motorcars shone in the sunlight, each one manned by driver in cap and stiffly starched jodhpurs. As the gate opened the ladies advanced as one, and a lone male, balding and rumpled, struggled to keep up with them.

From behind the fences of the Yard, Lena and Yvonne watched the gaggle as they were led towards the Keep.

"Who are they?" Lena asked.

"These would be the members of the *Ladies' Benevolent Female Reformation Society*... just a buncha harmless do-gooders... they come to visit once a month or so—just to check on our well-being. Make sure no bad men are taking advantage of us poor helpless girls... or maybe to hear some titillating stories about that kind of thing. It's hard to know which."

"Why?" Lena asked. "I mean why do they come here?"

"Some perceived sense of social guilt, who knows? Personally I figure they do it just to annoy their rich husbands. They bring the girls care

35

packages, pray with us, try to encourage us to be 'civil and ladylike' despite our conditions, blah blah..."

As the group of women disappeared inside the Administration Building, Lena looked up at the Warden's tower.

"And how do *they* feel about them?"

Yvonne shrugged. "The Wardens? I'm sure they'd just as soon see them gone, but I figure they don't have much choice. These broads are all the wives of the richest and most powerful men in the state. So if they want to play fairy godmother, they get to. Nobody in heaven or earth denies the rich their way. Not even *them*."

Far above the two women, in one of the windows of the tower, the heavy shutters were opened just the slightest bit. Eyes careful to avoid the light peered through them.

•　　•　　•

The room was a smaller antechamber to the Warden's main meeting room, though it was no cozier. The shuttered windows gave it an overwhelming gloom, but Miriam Chandler ignored it as she sat drinking tea along with Fenton Pollack, the State Correctional Supervisor. He wore a colorless, too-tight suit, and occasionally mopped beading sweat from his high forehead with a wrinkled handkerchief.

Warden Skelly sat behind his desk opposite them, watching them both with some impatience as he tapped his long fingers on the desktop: his nails making an unnerving series of *clack-clack-clack-clack* sounds. By all appearances Pollack was ready to bolt, unable to meet the Head Warden's gaze. But Miriam Chandler seemed wholly immune to the tension infusing the room. She simply kept drinking her tea until she was finished, then gently laid the cup and saucer on the table, wiping her mouth with a dainty (and pressed) handkerchief she then tucked back into her lacey sleeve.

Skelly had been waiting for her to finish before speaking. He'd been through this before.

"Mrs. Chandler, you were saying something about... therapy?"

"Yes, Warden. We women of the *LBFRS*, in speaking with some of the more enlightened minds in the area of female psychology and the study of female delinquency, have come to embrace the theory that the key to rehabilitating the female delinquent's mind and soul lies in constructive activity: working towards the betterment of her peers in the outside world, so to speak."

"Have you, now?" Skelly's form moved not even slightly.

"We have, in fact. What we're currently speaking to the Governor about is a step-process, whereby in addition to the usual physical recreation activities mandated by the prison system, there will be instituted a series of work-related therapies. Sewing, simple assembly tasks, that sort of thing. These activities will help the women feel like they are still a functional part of our society."

Skelly leaned back an inch in his tall chair: "I must confess, Mrs. Chandler... I simply don't see the point in rehabilitating women who will never again set foot outside this prison."

Mrs. Chandler stared the Warden down, completely unafraid. She had been forced to deal with this loathsome character for almost four years now, since her founding of the *Ladies' Benevolence* group. While others around her found Warden Skelly intimidating, even frightening, she simply found the man to be tiresome. His thinking was positively medieval, in keeping with this dungeon of a prison he ran. But the Head Warden held some kind of sway over the present Governor, as well as the one before him, and this gave him a degree of invulnerability that the Wardens of other prisons in the area did not enjoy. Miriam didn't remotely understand this sway, but she knew it meant that he was not going anywhere anytime soon. So she simply had to deal with the creature sitting opposite.

Pollock was twitching in his seat. The Warden and the lady had been locked in their staring match for almost a minute—neither willing to blink or back down. Finally, once more, Skelly's soft voice broke the silence.

"However, since our esteemed Honor the Governor obviously believes in the merits of your plan..."

Miriam nodded, triumphant. "He and I have spoken at great length about it."

"I see. Very well, when you have a schedule together, we will go about seeing how we may best implement these... therapies."

He rose, signaling that the meeting was over. Miriam and Pollock stood as well. The Warden towered over them in the small room.

"I'm sure you'd like to join your ladies and spend some time with our guests before you leave, Mrs. Chandler."

She stared up at him with steely, unafraid eyes: "I very much would. Would you care to walk out with me, Warden? Perhaps get some sun?"

Skelly's eyes darkened. He couldn't decide if the woman's request was innocent, or if it came loaded with meaning—and perhaps a subtle threat.

"I'm afraid some pressing reports will not afford me that privilege, madam."

She nodded. "I'll wish you a good day, then, Warden. Thank you for your time."

He bowed as they left. As they were walking out, Pollock couldn't help but cast a nervous glance back, and was chilled to see the cold ember of hatred burning in Warden Skelly's eyes as he stared at Miriam Chandler's retreating back. Then the doors shut.

●　　●　　●

The gaggle of women marched through the rows of cells. Guards hurried to get out of their way. Here and there one of the women would turn off, headed towards a specific destination in the prison. Their precision made it evident that they knew Steelegate's layout as well as any, and they had performed this choreography many times before.

●　　●　　●

Several girls knelt in the small prison chapel, praying along with the elderly Mrs. Hoffman, as she read from Holy Scripture:

"For the Lord has set a day when he will judge the world with justice by the man he has appointed... He has given proof of this to all men by raising him from the dead..."

Warden Smithfield betrayed a small sneer as he watched the women, all

38

the while being careful not to set foot within the chapel's threshold.

Down in the Laundry, women folded towels and sheets as usual, but today one sat apart, crying and being comforted by one of the *LBFRS* women. The guards shrugged at one another, knowing they were helpless to intervene.

Marguerite Vanderbosh sat at one of the Commissary tables, staring at Helen and Greta, who both sat across the table with arms folded, staring holes through her. Their talk was obviously not going well:

"Now, ladies—I want you to feel free to speak to me. Is anyone in this place... taking advantage of you as women?"

The two stared at her.

"What did you call us?"

The dainty woman stumbled, realizing her words.

"No, I-- I said 'as women'... I didn't- oh, my..."

The woman got up to leave. As she did, one of her companions—a younger woman named Stella Gabels, locked eyes momentarily with Greta. Mrs. Vanderbosh didn't see it, but Helen did, and smiled to herself.

•   •   •

Miriam Chandler and several other *LBFRS* ladies were watching over the girls in the Yard as they exercised.

"These poor girls," one of the women murmured, causing Miriam to turn on her with alacrity.

"Don't pity them," the leader remonstrated. "They are here because of their own poor choices."

"But——-"

The head woman stiffened: "The last thing you or I want is for women of this—inclination—to be roaming our streets. That said, there's no reason for them to be maltreated here. They're already paying their due to society."

She turned back to stare at the dozens of females in identical sack dresses.

"And of course, there's no reason they can't be made to be more useful to the rest of us while they're here, is there?"

No one present dared disagree.

•　　•　　•

Stella Gabels moved timidly through the changing room of the showers, looking all around her with wary eyes. It was empty. As she turned back, she ran right into Greta, who was waiting for her. Greta stared down at the dainty gentlewoman a moment, then without a word took her hand and led her into a secluded corner.

•　　•　　•

Lena was reading a dimestore novel Yvonne had already finished with, when a voice made her look up:

"Child?"

She saw a kindly elder woman was looking down at her through the open doorway.

"Hello." Lena said.

The woman came closer. "My name is Constance Chambers. What's your name?"

"Lena."

"That's such a pretty name... may I?"

She indicated the bunk next to her. Lena nodded and Mrs. Chambers sat down.

"Now then, you know who we are..."

"Yes, they told me. You come to look after us, make sure we're not being... mistreated."

"Exactly. Now I want you to know, anything you say to me is in the strictest confidence. I would never betray you to anyone should you choose to tell me about anything... inappropriate... that has happened to you, child."

"Okay..."

"So? Is there anything you feel you should share with me?"

Lena's eyes glanced past the woman's shoulder, catching a glimpse of one of the guards lurking just out of sight—listening.

40

"No. Nothing. I've only been here a week, but the guards have been very... decent to me."

Her ears caught the slightest clinking of the guard's keys as he wandered off, satisfied. Lena was sure the woman heard it as well.

"I see. I'm very glad to hear it. Please take care of yourself, Lena."

She stood up and turns to go.

"So have the Wardens." Lena said.

She could see Mrs. Chambers stiffen at the mention of the Prison's masters: "Well of course they have. I would expect little less."

She left, but Lena had witnessed the dread that came over the woman. The same chilling fear she felt at even the mention of the Wardens of Steelegate. She tried to pick up reading where she'd left off, but now found her mind wandering.

•   •   •

The sun was lowering as the women shuffled out through the prison gate to their idling autos.

As they left, several of the Wardens watched from a secluded arch inside.

"Time runs short for us, brothers..." Warden Kleig whispered. "Industry and invention make this country ever smaller... and these women, with their probing little minds and their sway over men's thoughts and pocketbooks... they are harbingers, signaling that our time is ending."

He turned to walked back into the shadows, and with a look, the others followed suit.

•   •   •

Warden Skelly watched the cars drive back down Cutback Pass from his window. The guard Reginald had entered behind him.

"Ladies are leaving, Warden."

"Yes, I can see, Reginald, thank you. Nothing... troubling... to report, I take it?"

"Nah. Girls know their place, sir."

"Yes. What say we give them an extra half-hour before lights out tonight?"

"Whatever you say, Warden."

He turned and left.

7.

7 November

IT WAS WARM TODAY, FOR November. Lena sat on a seat by the wall in the exercise yard, still reading her dimestore book. It wasn't very good, but it was allowing her to distract herself for a moment, at least. The story was about a young American woman brought to be a tutor for the adolescent heir of a wealthy English estate. Its gaudy prose vacillated between long, dull dialogues between the tutor lady and the boy's stern uncle, and lurid descriptions of her nocturnal liaisons with the estate's landscaper.

When someone sat down next to her on the bench, she didn't react for a bit. But as she reached the end of a chapter she glanced over—and her eyes widened in surprise.

It was Bonnie. She sat staring out absently into thin air. Her longish hair hung lank and stringy, covering most of her face. Her body swayed just a little as she sat, and she hummed a barely-audible melody to herself.

"Hi. It's Bonnie, right? My name is Lena. We didn't get a chance to meet before you were... before they took you away."

Receiving no response from the woman, she tried again.

"So they let you out of the Hole, huh?"

Now Bonnie finally turned to stare at her, and Lena got a good look. Bonnie's face was sunken, almost hollowed out: there were dark circles around both of her eyes, and her cheeks had caved in against the bones of her skull. The Hole had obviously been hell on her.

"Been a—a rough couple days for you, I guess, hasn't it?" But rather than replying, Bonnie began softly singing:

"In the deep, roused from sleep.

Now they come, no place to run..."

Lena reached out to touch the woman's shoulder: "Honey... are you alright?" her voice fell to a whisper: "What did they do to you down there?"

But as Lena's hand fell on her arm, Bonnie slapped it away violently.

"Hey, now! I was just trying to—"

But Bonnie had gone back to singing absently—a simple, old-fashioned melody, slightly off key:

"Three they come, have their fun.

Scream aloud, no one 'round.

Just a pinch, bleed an inch..."

Lena stared at her aghast as she sang. As they'd been sitting there, the lowering afternoon sun had moved just a bit, and its light had reached their legs. Lena's eyes caught Bonnie self-consciously moving back away from it.

"I have to go now. I have to see the Doctor," the pale girl whispered.

"Do you want me to take you there?" Lena asked.

Bonnie rose to her unsteady feet: "You're very kind. No, I can make my own way, thank you." And she tottered away, cautious to stay out of the direct light until she was back inside. As she did, Lena could still hear her singing quietly:

"Night by night, come to dine.

Eyes they shine, blood like wine..."

•　　•　　•

The prison was quiet later that evening. Lena and Yvonne sat on their respective bunks.

"How bad is the Hole?" Lena asked. She was certain she saw a shadow pass across Yvonne's face at the mention of it.

"Bad. You don't even want to know..."

"Actually I kinda do. That'd be why I asked about it."

Yvonne lay back on her bed, staring up at the underside of Lena's mattress, at her legs dangling off: "I've never been down there, luckily."

"But you've heard from girls who have. Like Bonnie."

"They said it's dark down there... like being buried alive... the rooms, they're like coffins... no window, no air... and they call it solitary, but... "

"But..?"

"But you're not alone down there. Do what they say, toe the line... and watch out for trouble... you don't have to go looking for it here, it'll find you, believe me."

The two reflected in silence for a bit before Lena spoke up again.

"How did you wind up in here, Yvonne?"

Yvonne rolled over on her bunk, facing the wall.

"Bad taste in men."

"Come on. You're a smart girl... you had some schooling, I can tell. And you have a good heart. You're decent to people, not like most of the rest here. What'd you do to get chucked into this hellhole?"

Yvonne reflected a moment, as if deciding whether to answer, and how much to tell.

"When the tough times hit, my husband—he stared working a lot of odd jobs: plumbing, pipefitting, parking cars... whatever he could to make a buck for us. He was an all-around alright guy. Not overly bright, but... he was good to me. And then he started doing jobs for this woman, this well-bred social registry type, with a husband who spent all his time up north."

"I think I can see where this is going..."

The woman on the lower bunk snorted.

"That's the big joke, isn't it? My story's so tired it doesn't have the legs to walk. Well, Bobby started doing more and more work for this lady... coming home late, sometimes not at all... the worst part is when everyone around you is in on the joke, but won't tell you the punchline, you know?"

"Yeah..."

"Well, one night when he didn't come home I decided to go up to her house to fetch him. Took me two hours walking to get there. When I did... there they were, in front of her fancy fireplace, all wrapped around each other."

She paused.

"My memory's not too good about what happened after. There was a fireplace poker, and then there was blood everywhere, and then the cops, and then—" She looked around her at the cell. "And then here I was... in Steelegate."

"How long ago was that?" Lena asked.

"Four years, come Spring."

Lena stared at the dark sky beyond their small window.

"It's not like I thought it'd be. This place, I mean. I thought it'd be scary... but it's more—just sad."

"Oh, it's got it's share of scary, honey... you just haven't seen the worst of it yet."

Lena bent down to stare at her cellmate below: "You talk about not being in on the joke. That's how it feels here... like you all know something I don't, and it's a real hoot."

"It's not a hoot, trust me. There's nothing funny about it at all."

"About what? What is it? What's wrong with this place?" she paused. "Besides the obvious, I mean."

The lights went out without warning. A guard walked past on the floor below, hollering:

"LIGHTS OUT! Everybody in her rack and quiet!"

Lena stared at Yvonne—now no more than a dark shape—for another moment, then laid back on her thin mattress. She lay there staring at the ceiling, then finally spoke up again, quietly.

"Helen had another name for this place. She called it Bloodsucker City. What did she mean?"

Yvette's response came disembodied out of the black: "You're not ready to know... not yet. Soon, though... soon you won't have a choice."

•　　•　　•

Dottie stood alone in the shower room, enjoying the feeling of the lukewarm spray from one of the nozzles on her shoulders. The water cascaded over her body in rivulets and dripped off her curves to spatter at her feet on

46

the tile floor below.

Lost in the moment, she seemed almost to not hear the sound of approaching boots as they grew louder and louder.

A nightstick dragged against the tile walls, clicking off each individual tile block as its owner came closer and closer to the showering woman. Finally Dottie threw a glance over her shoulder to see the slender guard standing there, looking her body over from head to toe. Her hand reached out on its own and turned off the shower. The room grew quiet as she stood there before him, dripping.

"Oh... hi."

The guard frowned: "You realize it's after lights out, don't you? Prisoners aren't allowed out of their racks at this hour."

"I guess I must have not heard the bell."

He came a small step closer to her.

"Us guards, we find a prisoner breaking the rules, they say we can use our own discretion as to what kind of punishment to mete out."

Her eyebrow rose.

"Do they?"

"They do. So what kind of punishment do you think you deserve?"

She smiled. This was a game they were playing, and they'd played it many times before: "I have a few ideas... they all take a while. That okay?"

"I'm covered. Now you gonna tell me what those three girls are up to, or do you want to wait until... after?"

"How about—after?"

"Duck Soup," he smiled, and Dottie knelt down before him. Her fingers tugged at the buttons on the front of his woolen trousers.

8.

THE LAUNDRY WAS A LOWER-LEVEL affair. It was adjacent to the boiler room, so between the dryers and the furnaces, the space was stiflingly hot even in the coldest months.

It was a vast space, bigger than it needed to be, really: with a soaring, vaulted ceiling thirty feet above. A single, rickety staircase with several landings led up the near wall to an iron door accessing the hallway above. There was no other exit. What its original purpose when the prison had first been built was a mystery—maybe it had been the powder magazine, or perhaps it was used for flour and grain storage. But now it housed seven hulking stainless steel industrial washing machines and a half-dozen dryers of equally massive size, each one as big as a Buick. The washers ran in two rows, one against the outer wall, one along the inner; and the dryers were lined up back-to-back down the center. This took up about half the room—the rest was filled with a myriad of clotheslines for articles unsuited to mechanized drying like undergarments; and ironing stations for those articles which required a more finished look. Everything washable was the same dull shade of greyish white. Not a single piece—clothing, bedding, tablecloth or napkin—bore any color. This was intentional, and it was strictly enforced.

On this day, a Tuesday, in and amongst these giant machines worked some twenty or twenty-five women prisoners, each stripped down to the barest clothing permitted, yet still dripping in sweat. They worked in pairs: some

48

hurtling great armfuls of soiled linens into the washers, while other teams pulled the laundered items out, loading the wet white clumps into rolling wire baskets to pile in front of the dryers, where still more teams peeled them apart, shaking out any remaining water before tossing them in to be dried. If it wasn't a completely efficient organization, it was at least orderly.

A tarnished bell mounted by the exit door clapped loudly three times, and the women—by long practice and programming—all simultaneously dropped whatever it was they were currently occupied with and moved into line, many of them grabbing up their threadbare dresses to cover up before going upstairs.

Guard Barlowe blew three quick shrill notes on his whistle, and the tired sweaty line began shuffling up the steps. The man's eyes watched each woman as she passed carefully, and as the end of the line neared, his billy club came up: blocking Helen, Greta and Big Hallie, who were bringing up the rear.

"Hold up there just a minute..."

The three women obliged, halting. They glanced up at him, but mostly stared at the floor, occasionally flashing a look at one of the others, until another guard named William came up.

"This them?"

"Yeah."

William brought himself to his full height of five-and-one-half-feet. "Okay, ladies. Let's see those hands."

"Excuse me?" Helen stared the guard down.

Behind their backs, all three were subtly wiping off their hands on their rears.

"Gotta make sure." Barlowe grunted.

The girls look at each other and offer their hands. The guards scanned them, and the one gave the other a nod.

"Okay, get going, then..."

Without another word the three headed up the stairs. William gave Barlowe a subtle nod, and the other glanced at their dirt-streaked hindquarters as they hurried up. The two men shared a confident nod, then followed the women up, leaving behind the vast empty room with its silent machines, its dirty laundry, and a small pile of fine dust under the back corner of one of the machines facing the interior wall.

Helen, Greta and Hallie followed the single file line towards the commissary. Helen checked to make sure no one was near enough to overhear.

"Someone's ratting us out, ladies..."

Greta stared down the row of women in front of them. "Who do you think it is?"

"I don't know yet, but I will."

They filed through the serving line, getting their allotment of bland, colorless food. All the time their eyes searched the rows of women, and the guards watching them, while avoiding the unnerving eyes of Warden Kleig; who stood, motionless, at the far end of the dining room.

As the three carried their half-full trays to their seats they passed Dottie, who leaned over her food inconspicuously, all the while following them with her eyes. A tiny smile cracked across her face as they passed her by.

The girls sait, peering all around them for anyone suspicious.

"What about Bonnie? Maybe she's got a grudge after our little fracas..."

They peered over at the girl, who sat a bit off from the group, in a daze, her fork halted in midair halfway to her mouth, applesauce spilling off of it.

Greta snorted. "You're kidding, right? She's still got the shivers from the Hole—doesn't look like they're going away anytime soon, either."

"So? Better her than me, right?" Big Hallie mumbled while shoveling bites into her mouth.

The slender woman shrugged: "If you say so.'

Hallie had had enough. "You better start appreciating what I bring to our little arrangement, pipsqueak... without me how are you gonna—?"

They both got a look from Helen.

"You both wanna clam up, or should I just send a telegram to the Wardens about our little enterprise?"

"Sorry."

"Sorry."

The three settled into a silence as they ate, until Greta, taking a bite of creamed potatoes, subtly nodded across the way.

"Take a gander over at Yvonne."

The others look up.

Yvonne sat next to Lena, sipping coffee from a steel mug. As they watched they saw her nod almost imperceptibly to one of the younger guards, an eager-to-please type whom the other guards jokingly called "Manners".

Manners gave her the most minimal of nods back, pretending to check his pocket watch—tapping it like he was checking the function of its working, and then he subtly held up one finger.

Yvonne went back to drinking her coffee.

Greta gave out a low whistle. "It's her. It's gotta be her."

"Funny, she's always been an upright dame... guess it's always who you least suspect, isn't it? Shame."

"What do we do?" Big Hallie asked.

Helen considered between bites of soggy cornbread. "We watch her, and we wait for our moment—then we make sure she won't rat on us or anyone else any more."

She went back to digging into her dinner.

• • •

A row of sagging wooden stalls lined the tiled floor space of the West Lavatory. The place was forever dripping and damp, with the sharp stinging smell of lye covering up the more pungent odor of sewage lurking underneath. Above, the filament of a single bare bulb in a tiny wire cage flickered, managing to leave the room dimly lit despite its glare.

Manners looked up at it as he entered timidly, only to be rewarded with a drop of mucky water from the ceiling in his eye.

"Gaa—is anyone in here?"

Down the line, a toilet flushed, and Yvonne strolled out of the stall.

"A true moment of privacy's a rare thing in here..."

Manners shifted nervously. He checked behind him to make sure no one else was present. "I... I got what you asked for from the storage."

Acting coy, Yvonne made a deal of fussing with a stray lock of her dark hair.

"Good. May I have it?"

51

"You said... you said you'd—"

"Yes, I remember. Come here."

The boy took a step closer, then moved forward quickly, forgetting himself as she pulled out a rolled-up comic book from behind her back.

"Here: lucky you, I got the wrong gift package from the Ladies this month."

Manners snatched it up and carefully unfurled it, staring at the cover with its bright primary colors. A blue-clad muscle man battled green and grey alien foes against a cadmium yellow background.

"My mama doesn't let me—I mean, this one's hard to find. Drug store in town don't carry it." He stood engrossed in the comic, until Yvonne quietly coughed.

"Oh. Right. Here."

He absently handed her a folding photo case, brushed metal on the outside, with a small inscription.

"Had to take the glass out, because, you know... but the pic's still in there."

"Thanks hon, you're a doll. Gotta go, it's almost curfew."

She turned, but then paused a moment to turn back and wink: "See you in the funny papers."

Even as she left, he was still reading.

•   •   •

Exiting the washroom, Yvonne checked left and right down the hallway. Seeing no one, she hurried back towards her block, passing right by Greta, who stood in a small shadowed declivity in the wall.

After a moment Manners came out too, buttoning up his wool blouse where he'd stashed the comic—equally wary and equally ignorant of Greta's presence. He hurried off in the opposite direction towards the guard shack in the West Tower.

Greta's face darkened. She gave them both another moment to disappear, then hurried off herself.

9.

LENA HAD COME BACK FROM the Commissary, ready for lights out in a few minutes. But as she entered her cell, her eyes fixed on something sitting on her shelf.

A tiny picture frame, and in it a black and white photo of her holding her son.

She turned to stare at Yvonne, who lay in her bunk, casually reading.

Lena couldn't make her words work: "What..? They took this when— How did you..?"

Yvonne gave a yawn.

"Do me a favor and don't make a big scene about it, alright? I just thought—you're a nice gal and you're stuck in here with all us bad eggs... and you were kind about how I got in here."

She slowly stood.

"I guess this is just me saying... I know you didn't kill your boy. And I'm sorry you ain't got him anymore."

Lena's arms encircled Yvonne in an instant, and she hugged the other woman tightly. The tears came, unbeckoned.

She whispered: "Thank you."

Yvonne suffered Lena's embrace for a moment, fighting back her own long-dormant emotions, until she couldn't take it anymore.

"Alright, get off..."

Lena smiled. She took the small picture off her shelf, clutching it to her breast. This was everything. They'd taken so much from her, but she had this back now. She could survive this. She climbed up to her bunk and lay down, staring at the photo, re-memorizing every contour of Jonathan's face. She could remember it all again. His voice. His scent. She had him back.

She still clutched it as her eyes closed.

•　　•　　•

Far above the cellblock, Warden Skelly sat at the table in the Wardens' Office, his long fingers entwined. Manners stood before him, shaking with fear.

•　　•　　•

The attack came the next day.

The women were in line as they walked down a hallway—a guard at either end escorting them. Greta and Helen were near the front, and Lena and Yvonne were in the middle, several people behind them. Greta and Helen were both cautiously moving up through the line, getting closer to the front guard.

In the back by the rear guard, Hallie waited for Helen's signal.

Manners was the one up front leading them: "In accordance with the new State guidelines, you ladies are gonna be learning a productive trade so y'all can be better parts of society... or something. So if your mamas never taught you to sew, well you're gonna learn now."

Helen was waiting for a certain moment. When she sensed it was there, she nodded to Greta, and turned back to nod to Hallie.

Hallie took a big step to her left, blocking the rear gGuard's view with her bulk. The man bellowed "Hey! Move it, fatty!"

While his view was blocked, Greta reached a lighting fast hand out and snatched Manners' billy club out from its holster, delivering a nasty blow to the back of his head. The young man never had a chance to turn around before he went down with a cry. In a flash, Greta turned and tossed the stick to Yvonne's feet, stepping back in line.

Hallie immediately moved aside and the rear Guard's eyes went wide, seeing his partner on the ground and Yvonne standing by his weapon.

"Hey! HEY!" he screamed, and charged forward even as the younger guard struggled to one knee, holding his head.

Helen pointed at Yvonne, yelling: "She just went crazy!"

"Why would you do that?" Greta's voice barely concealed her mocking enjoyment.

Yvonne stared at the club at her feet, at the guard rising, his partner charging. Her eyes swung to Helen and Greta:

"You goddamn LIARS!"

She shoved past Lena and started to go for them, but Lena held her back.

"No! It's what they want!"

Yvonne's fury passed in an instant. She knew her friend was right, and raised her hands up, kicking the stick towards the guard.

"Manners, you know I didn't do it. It was those two."

The rear guard looked at Manners, but he shook his head.

"I didn't see."

He snatched up the stick and tried to balance on his shaky feet. His young face was contorted in anger.

"Someone's going in the Hole for a helluva long time for that... now who did it? WHO!?"

Lena looked around. The other girls were all staring at the floor, afraid to talk.

Manners nodded. "I see... no witnesses, huh? Fine:"

He reached out and grabbed Yvonne by the blouse, but in an instant Lena was pushing herself between them.

"No! It was me!"

Yvonne spun on her. "What are you doing?"

"It's not fair—they set you up."

"Yeah. Me. Not you." She spoke loudly. "It was me, not her!"

Helen chimed in: "Yeah, it was her!"

Manners stared at both of them. He raised his nightstick, and Yvonne and Lena both tensed. They could see him silently mouthing *eeny-meenie-miney-moe*, until he finally ended pointing at Lena. Without a word he brought the stick around and smacked her in the stomach, doubling her over. She collapsed to the ground.

Yvonne screamed "NO!" and lunged at Manners, but was rewarded by a jab to the eye with the stick. She stumbled back.

"You manage this lot?" Manners asked his partner, who nodded. The young guard grabbed Lena by the hair and began dragging her away.

"Cooling your heels in The Hole for a few days should take the spunk outta you, sister..."

As she was hauled past Helen and Greta and Hallie, Lena could see them watching her go with mixed enjoyment and annoyance. She could feel clumps of hair tearing free from her scalp as she was pulled, and the tile ground scraped painfully on her hips. Then they finally reached the far end of the hallway: she was pulled through and the door slammed shut behind them.

Yvonne struggled to get up on one knee, holding her bruised eye socket, only to see Helen staring down at her.

"Happy?" she asked.

Helen just stared down at her with hatred.

"You'll get yours... meanwhile, we got sewing to do."

The guard yelled at them to get moving, and Yvonne and the others fell back in line.

•　　•　　•

Lena was led by the arm through a series of stairs, hallways, walkways and catwalks—- down, down, down into lower regions of the prison she'd not yet seen. After a point, she was sure they must have passed well below ground level, and that the passageways she was treading were hewn into the very rock of the mountain Steelgate perched upon.

The place seemed to get older as they went down, as well. The stones were larger; their assembly into walls and flooring was cruder, as if it these passages had been made before the advent of modern tools. It almost felt like going backwards in time. This deep, Steelgate also seemed in much worse repair than above—groundwater leaked through cracks in the ceiling, dripping on her head and pooling in the uneven stone at her feet.

After what seemed like a long way, Manners led her down a final set of steep steps into a narrow passageway with three steel doors on one side, and then pulled her to a stop.

"Strip down to your undergarment. Shoes too."

Lena complied, pulling off her sack dress and stepping out of her shoes. The stone ground was cold under her feet. She carefully folded her dress and laid her articles on a small bench the guard indicated.

Manners pulled out his key ring, sifting through the dozens of keys until finding a particularly ancient-looking one. He slipped this key into the lock on the near door, and using some effort, he pulled. The door opened with a quiet shriek of metal scraping against metal.

Lena took several tentative steps into a narrow and completely bare cell. Manners entered behind her. For the first time since the altercation, Lena felt a real, tangible fear suffuse through her body, and she realized she'd made a mistake. She was alone and completely vulnerable down here. She turned to face the man standing there staring at her, ready for anything that might be coming. But she was confused to see only a strange look of sympathy on his young face.

"You got yourself three whole days down here. No light. No bed. No yard time. One meal a day and a hole in the corner... and trust me—that's nowhere near the worst part of it."

Manners came a bit closer, and Lena tensed.

"I know it wasn't you hit me."

Lena didn't know what to say: "So why—?"

"Helen and those others... they got guards on their side. I send one of them down here, and I queer myself with those guys, and that'd make working here... difficult. So I'm sorry. Someone had to go down to the Hole, and you just put yourself in the wrong place, I guess."

"Yeah. Okay,." wWas all Lena said. Nothing she could say was going to change anything anyway. She was going to be stuck here.

Reaching into his pocket, Manners pulled out a crudely-made shiv: really just a half-sharpened piece of metal with a rag-wrapped handle, perhaps six inches long in total. She stared at it.

"You seem like a pretty nice lady. Maybe you had a reason to kill your kid."

"I didn't—"

"Like I said, maybe you had a reason. I don't know... but now you're stuck down here... all alone... where no one'll hear you scream..."

Lena backed up nervously, eyeing the blade in his hand.

"You been here a bit now... you know things ain't quite right in this place."

When she replied, her voice came out hoarse: "I... yeah."

Manners looked into her eyes, then down at the blade—and offered it to her, handle first.

She stared at it, at him, unsure.

"It's a one-time offer. Take it, and take care of yourself now. It'll be better than what's comin' for you down here in the dark."

She stared at the crude blade in horror. He really wanted her to do it.

"I'll say you pulled it out before I could search you. You threatened me, then cut your wrists before I could stop you."

She stared at the boy's face, thinking how he was barely older than Jonathan, really. A few years. Five, seven at most.

"I—why are you doing this?"

"Maybe cause I don't wanna come back down here in a couple days and see what they left of you."

"They?" awareness—true awareness, was slowly dawning in the back of her mind.

"You really haven't figured it out yet, have you? You poor dumb ignorant lady... you take it and take care of yourself, or you'll be sorry, I promise."

She stared at the knife for another moment, then stepped back.

"Take it away."

Manners tucked the blade back into his pocket without another word.

"Fine. Suit yourself. But I promise: after tonight, you're gonna wish you did."

He turned and strode out of the cell. The steel door slammed shut behind him. Lena heard the key turn the bolt, and then his footsteps fading away as he mounted the steps and left her all alone.

10.

1 December

LENA TURNED 'ROUND AND 'ROUND in the small claustrophobic cube. It was very dark. The only feeble light came a narrow shaft glancing from under the door. The solitary cell was cave-like: it seemed to have been hewn out of solid rock, rather than built. One entire wall was covered with a dark green mossy growth that reeked like sulfur and ran a ways onto the floor. There was no commode, only a small circular hole in the corner right of the door.

She squatted down in the corner, pulling her bruised knees up to her chin and hugging her bare legs in the dark.

•   •   •

Above, the sun had just lowered below the high brick walls of the prison courtyard.

Warden Skelly was watching the last light of the day decay away from behind the safety of his shutters. He was aware of the other Wardens waiting patiently in the room behind him, but chose to savor the moment and make them wait a little longer. It would be good for them and besides: this was his favorite moment of the day—the moment it ended.

Finally, as the sky forsook its orange tint and took on an azure cast, he turned.

"Yes?"

It was Kleig who spoke up: "We're waiting for your word, Warden."

"Ah, yes. Forgive me. Just three of you, please."

Warden Tarker looked surprised. "You don't—?"

But Skelly raised a long bony hand. "No, thank you..."

He turned back to contemplate the growing darkness outside as, without another word, the shapes behind him turned and exited.

●　●　●

Lena lay curled up on the hard floor, her eyes shut but unable to sleep in the cold, hard conditions. The light from under the door had faded, so she knew that somewhere outside, it was night.

There had been no sound, but she'd sensed something. She wasn't alone: something was in the cell with her.

She was up in a second, retreating back into her corner.

"Who's here?"

She squinted in the gloom, trying to pick out a shape: a furtive movement, anything. The briefest shifting of a shadow caught her eye; then it was gone.

"Who are you? What do you want with me?"

There came the faintest chuckle from the darkness.

Lena felt herself growing more and more panicked, but fought with all her might to quell it: "You afraid of me? Huh? Are you? Then quit hiding and let me see you, already!"

But then her voice faltered, as suddenly she realized that her visitor was *right next to her*. She could barely make out the black-draped figure with its bald head, hawkish features, and shining eyes.

It was Warden Kleig.

He whispered in her ear: "Shhhhhhhhhhhhhhhhh... not so much noise in so small a space, please..." This close she could feel his breath was cold as the tomb, and just as rotten. Lena found herself paralyzed with fear. She couldn't make herself move.

60

"Wha—what?"

A long-fingered hand reached up and ever-so delicately covered her mouth: "No talking now..."

Her eyes moved down as the other hand reached to gently grab her bare thigh, gently squeezing until she winced at his pinch.

"If you are quiet... if you do not fight... this will be over quickly, and we will be gone..."

She looked around with new terror: "*We*"?

Even as she whispered the words, two more shapes seemed to materialize out of the dark recesses of the cell: Warden Tarker, and Warden Tolifson. They both crawled across the floor towards her on all fours, bellies flattened against the stones like feral creatures.

She was sure she knew what was coming: she was about to be gang raped. This was why the girls would only whisper about the Hole. This was why Bonnie had come back barely sane. This was what they did. This was Steelegate's dark secret.

She could feel tears cascading down her face. "No... please..."

Kleig's sibilant whisper sounded in her ear again:

"Begging is futile, child... now hush, and close your eyes..."

In the black she could feel the others swarm silently over her, spreading her arms and legs wide. Her entire body was absolutely shaking with fear.

Lena closed her eyes as tears poured down her cheeks. She felt cold breath on her throat, on the delicate flesh of her inner arm, against the sensitive skin of her upper thigh. Then she felt the needle-like stings. Her face contorted in pain and she cried out and tried to wrench free, but it was impossible. Very quickly the shapes and contours before her became liquid and diffused. Darkness grew around the edges of her periphery and swept towards the center—then in the void all she could hear was the echoes of her own gasping.

•　　•　　•

Above, the prison was quiet. The commissary, laundry and courtyards sat empty, and the usual soft sounds of snoring, moans and tears were barely audible tonight. A lone guard wandered the block, swinging his stick: his shoes making the only sound.

• • •

The sun rose over the surrounding swamps and hills.

A tiny blade of diffused light streamed under the doorway to Lena's cell, but nevertheless she squinted at its dim luminescence. Her narrowed eyes were hollow, and haunted. The hours of the day passed in a daze as she watched the shadows that lurked in the dark corners of her room, waiting patiently.

• • •

Yvonne was on her hands and knees in the showers, scrubbing the stained tile floor with a scrub brush. This was her punishment for her part in the nightstick incident. She'd done the north bath last night, and the west lavatory was her task this evening. A guard had been posted to watch her, and as she'd worked away the last hour and a half, she'd occasionally heard the man shifting impatiently, bored at his task.

But as Yvonne paused to wipe the sweat from her face, she sensed that something had changed. Turning, she saw that the guard was gone—and Helen and Greta stood between her and the exit.

"Oh. Swell. I was having such a good day, I was afraid nobody would show up to ruin it..."

Helen came a few inches closer: "We're gonna have a little talk with you."

Yvonne glanced from one woman to the other.

"Gonna be one of those two-on-one talks, is it?"

The tall girl sneered: "I know a little girl who needs to learn some respect for the order of things..."

"And I know a little girl who needs to be back in her cell by the dinner bell, so if you'll excuse me, ladies?" Yvonne was trying to gauge the danger of the situation. Her instincts told her that there was some kind of cipher lurking here—a missing part of the equation that she couldn't calculate. She started to walk past them, but Greta grabbed her dress and shoved her back into the center of the room.

"She said we were gonna have a discussion," the dark-skinned girl said. "Maybe you didn't hear that part?"

Yvonne was slowly backing towards the wall, hoping to put her back against it when the attack came. Helen and Greta followed her step for step.

"Okay, but just so you both know—I'm not going to the infirmary alone..."

Her back bumped up against the tile. She had nowhere left to go. It was coming soon. She nodded to the others.

"Did you ladies want to air your grievances before we begin?

"It's come to my attention that certain plans of ours have become common knowledge to certain other girls... Greta here saw you being friendly with that new guard, the young'n."

"Well, Greta here is an idjit... and besides that, she's also wrong."

Greta's face was close to hers: "So you don't know anything about, say... a tunnel?

"If I did I'd keep it to myself. Of course, now I do know about it, thanks to you two geniuses."

The other two looked at one another.

"Same thing applies, though. You gals don't have to worry. I can keep my mouth shut."

Greta's hands were tightening into fists.

"Or we could shut it. For good."

"You've watched too many nickel gangster movies, doll."

Helen shook her head: "This is getting us nowhere."

Greta smiled: "Agreed."

Yvonne looked at them both a second—and shrugged.

"Agreed."

She lashed out, whacking Greta upside the head with the wooden scrub brush. The tall girl went down on one knee from the impact. Helen's left hand snatched out and grabbed Yvonne by the throat, her right hand punching her in the face once, twice. Yvonne felt the knuckles connecting with her cheek with blinding pain—it seemed like she could feel every small bone and piece of cartilage breaking with each impact.

On the third swing she managed to duck and Helen's fist connected with the tiled wall. As the girl gasped and grabbed her bruised knuckles, Yvonne lowered her shoulder and plowed into her, knocking her to the hard floor.

But now Greta had recovered, and she reached out and grabbed Yvonne from behind in a headlock. The taller, stronger girl spun Yvonne around with ease on the slippery floor, bashing her face into the wall several times with jarring intensity.

Yvonne's body was working on pure instinct at this point. She braced her foot on the wall and kicked back, knocking them both over. She landed hard on top of Greta, knocking the wind out of her.

In a flash Yvonne had flipped over so she was straddling her, and, grabbing Greta by the ears, began bashing the back of her head off the floor several times—until the woman's hands had stopped flailing.

Yvonne sat back, gasping, wiping away the blood that ran freely from her nose: but then Helen dropped a towel over her head and yanked back, cutting off her air. She was dragged across the floor as Greta stumbled towards her. Greta's legs were shaky, but she still managed to land several shattering blows to Yvonne's torso and face. Helen's voice came to Yvonne's ears through gritted teeth: "I believe I was saying something about the natural order of things..."

None of the three could see that, from one of the shadows, Warden Evers was watching the entire struggle with detached interest.

Greta continued to pummel Yvonne, her knuckles now covered in the girl's blood.

"Told you, we got a plan... got no time for nobody to wreck it now... too much at stake... I'm NOT gonna die in this place... Not gonna die."

"That's enough," Helen warned her, but Greta kept swinging, hitting Yvonne again and again, until finally Helen grabbed her swinging fist, stopping her. Yvonne's face was a bloody mess beneath them.

"ENOUGH!"

Greta stared, as she seemed to see the ruin below her for the first time.

"I didn't... I was just—"

"Put a lid on it. Come on, we gotta make tracks. We can't get caught here with her."

They both stood, staring at each other's blood-covered limbs.

"Shower."

They hurried to one of the nozzles, turning on the faucet and standing under the spray, washing the blood off.

"It's not coming—""

"Don't even say it. Come on, that's good enough. It's almost lights out, hurry up."

The two women grabbed towels, drying themselves off, and Helen took Greta's hand to pull her out of the room. As they exited, they passed right by Warden Evers.

"We don't EVER talk about this, even to each other. NEVER. It never happened, you understand?"

Greta nodded, struggling to keep up. She'd taken her share of pounding.

"I'm not a goddamn idiot..."

"Yeah? Sometimes I really wonder."

It was several moments after their voices and footsteps had faded, that the Warden emerged from the shadows. He slowly approached Yvonne, who lay on her back in the center of the room, choking on her own blood. He was taking his time, pausing to stare down at her. Then, slowly, he knelt down by her side.

Yvonne stared upward at the ceiling: one eye was already swollen closed. The other was blood-blind. Her jaw was cracked, her words coming out in a slur.

"Pleash... I need... help... pleash..."

Warden Evers reached slowly down, picking up her battered head and cradling it gently. He was enjoying prolonging this.

Yvonne could only feel the touch at first: "Thank... thank you... I—I thought—" but then as she stared, her intact eye managed to focus a bit, and she realized who it was that knelt over her.

"No... no... no, pleash!"

Warden Evers smiled, revealing rows of razor sharp teeth that seemed to protrude even further out of his gums as he widened his mouth. In a moment, he'd buried them in her neck with a crunch of flesh and sinew and bone.

Yvonne thrashed weakly in his steel grip, kicking at the air, helpless, as he drained her of her blood.

●　　●　　●

The little light that leaked under the door had dimmed to almost nothing now that night had fallen. In the near-total darkness, Lena sat huddled in a corner, hugging her knees.

She looked up as she heard, very faintly, a far-off scream, which quickly faded back into silence.

Even as it did, she was suddenly aware of shapes moving in the darkness near her. She had nowhere to go. She huddled against the hard, damp wall as they came closer and closer.

●　　●　　●

The sun rose over the distant hills.

Lena was curled up on the floor hugging her knees, weeping quietly. Tiny, shuddering sobs that made her entire body shake.

In her mind's eye she saw flashes of her life with her boy: *they were sitting at the table eating spaghetti and laughing. She was helping him with his schoolwork. She was tucking him into bed, kissing his head. She was cradling his dead body, screaming as the door burst open behind her and police rushed in, grabbing her and pulling her away from him as she fought them.*

She opened her eyes, and saw Jonathan standing there in the dim light of the cell, staring at her.

She reached out weakly to him, whispering: "Jonathan... honey..."

In a flash her eyes opened for real. She struggled to raise her head and look around her.

Her son was gone. Forever.

She curled back up.

11.

3 December

THE DOOR TO LENA AND Yvonne's cell was yanked open, and Lena's limp body was dragged inside by the guards Michael and Miles, and dropped onto the hard floor. The door rattled closed behind her.

"You see her eyes?"

"Christ, they're getting greedier... used to be it'd take two, three times in the Hole before they looked like that..."

Lena lay there, listening to the blurred voices of the guards as they walked away.

"Something's changing, ain't it?"

"Boy, you ain't kidding."

Their low voices went away as they went off down the corridor to their next task, and Lena's gaze moved around the cell, trying to make the world come into focus. It was all a blur: the shapes of the bunks, the toilet and the shelves all struggled to resolve themselves into a clear picture in her mind. But finally with some effort, they did. And as they did, something caught her eye, and she struggled to her shaky feet.

She teetered over to the far wall, having to grab it at the last minute to support herself. She negotiated her way over to Yvonne's shelf, and peered into it.

It was empty. Lena turned and realized her cellmate's blanket was gone as well, revealing the naked mattress.

Lena stared at it, her eyes tearing up.

"No... no...' She crawled into the bare bunk, curling up.

"Noo... no....." she whimpered, until exhaustion eventually took her over.

●　　●　　●

Her eye opened at the sound of the Breakfast Bell, immediately blinking and squinting at the light from outside. She was still lying on Yvonne's bed.

Slowly she raised her hand to block out the light.

●　　●　　●

All the women sat eating a slurried hash with hard bread. All but Lena, who sat staring at her tray. The unappetizing food sitting on it revolted her, and she pushed it away.

Helen, Greta and Big Hallie were escorted into the room along with several others who'd been in the sewing program. Two Lena noticed tof the three hey both had bruises on their faces, Lena noticed.

After a second she sensed eyes resting upon her, and looked up to see Warden Oberlun up front, watching her from a shadowed alcove.

She stared back at him, and the creature smiled ever-so-slightly.

●　　●　　●

Lena sat undressed on the cold steel table as Doctor Mears examined her with her accustomed dispassion.

"You're in decent shape, considering..."

"Considering what?"

The woman stared at her through her thick glasses, then pulled Lena's arm out to reveal the raw bite marks on the tender flesh inside of her elbow.

"Considering what I imagine you've been through the last seventy-two hours."

There was silence for a moment as the physician continued her exam.

Finally Lena had to ask: "How can you do this?"

"Raise your arms," the Doc requested, then seemed to sigh: "It's my job."

"But you know what happens down there."

"Don't be silly. Of course I do. I do the post-mortem on all the bodies that leave here."

Lena leaned forward, fighting to catch the other woman's eyes. "So you must know what they are... there's a name for it—"

"Don't. Don't say it out loud."

She glanced over her shoulder.

"They don't like it to be said out loud... And they have excellent hearing."

She placed the chilly stethoscope to the flesh of Lena's chest, "You don't really understand anything of how this works."

"I've had some pretty close experience lately..."

"And I'm sorry. I really am. But you girls put yourselves in this place. If you'd behaved yourselves out there, you'd have never ended up in here. If this... this evil has to happen, well then—better it happen to your lot than all the innocent people out there. You asked me how I can justify this? That's how."

"Would it matter to you if I told you that I was innocent? That I didn't kill my son?"

The DDoctor sighed again as she pulled the stethoscope's earpieces out, "That's what you all say."

Lena impulsively reached grabbed her hand, "My son had bled almost to death by the time I got home. But there was almost no blood on the floor. Nobody ever asked how that could happen... Where it could have gone." She had Mears' eyes locked now, "What does that sound like to you, Doctor?"

Doctor Mears returned Lena's gaze for a moment, seeming almost to want to believe her—then: "That sounds like an unfortunate coincidence... for you."

Lena's eyes fell. "They're monsters... they're creatures of—darkness... but you're a living, breathing person. A woman."

The DDoctor once more looked over her shoulder towards the door, making certain.

"You think I enjoy this? Working so hard to keep you all healthy, all the time knowing what's going to happen to each and every one of you in the end? The utter pointlessness of what I spend my days doing? Lay back."

Lena obeyed.

"Then why not quit? Why not go to the police?"

The DoctorDr. Mears chuckled even as she raised Lena's legs to check her pelvis. "Don't be naïve. You spent some time with the local police. Just how helpful do you think they'd be?"

"The *state* police, then. Someone who isn't under their sway."

"That would be a long drive, young lady, trust me. And if I did, what would I tell them, hmm?"

Lena realized she was right.

Mears lowered her legs again. "Exactly. They'd put me in a cell, too, and hire someone else to attend you girls. Would you like to hear some stories about the last guy that worked in this clinic? Trust me, you don't. You can get dressed."

Lena sat up, pulling her tunic back on as the Doctor sat down on her stool, filling out a form on a clipboard.

"How long?"

The Doc looked up: "How long what?"

"How long have they been here... doing this?"

The Doctor rolled over, swabbing Lena's arm and charging a hypodermic needle with clear fluid.

"You probably heard, this prison's built on the foundation of a Confederate fort from the Civil War. There are tunnels underneath that were used during the American Revolution. Before the white man ever came here the local Choctaw Indians had a name for the caves those tunnels were carved from, and they stayed well clear of them. I think you get my drift, right?"

"Yeah."

Doctor Mears jabbed her with the syringe, making her wince.

"Okay, now—you're dehydrated and malnourished. I've given you a vitamin shot but it's going to take a week or so of good eating and fluids to get you fully back to good health. I know eating's the last thing you feel like doing after... the last few days, but it's the best way for your body to recover."

Lena nodded, hesitating to ask, but then: "And the sunlight?"

The older woman frowned.

"The sensitivity to light should pass over the next few days, too. You've—taken on a few of their characteristics... some small exchanging of the bodily fluids during... the act. But you're young and reasonably fit: you'll feel more yourself soon."

Lena looked out the window at the bright sunlight coming in: "Sunlight..."

"They can tolerate it in small doses, but they don't like it one bit, let me tell you."

Lena swung back to the Doc, "Someone's got to stop all this. It can't just keep going on and on..."

"You're not thinking straight. You're angry and hurt. I understand. But if you'd been here as long as I have, you'd realize..."

"What?"

Mears sat back. "That things just are the way they are. It's not fair. But it's the way it is."

Lena couldn't abide that.

"It doesn't have to be. You don't have to keep doing this... fattening us up for the slaughter. You can help me get out."

"They know exactly where my house is. They know where my husband works. They know what school my children go to and exactly which upstairs bedroom they sleep in," she paused, "No. I can't help you."

Lena nodded, and got up to leave. She made it a few steps before Doctor Mears' voice halted her:

"If I were you, I'd be on my best behavior the next few weeks. You wouldn't survive another trip down to the Hole right now, trust me. Now go get some food."

Lena smiled without humor or thanks.

"Right. Thanks a heap, Doc."

She walked out, leaving the Doctor staring at her notes in silence.

12.

THE NEXT FEW WEEKS PASSED largely without incident. True to the doctor's promise, Lena found that eating was helping her feel more human again, bit by bit. In fact—and it might have been all in her head—she actually felt stronger than she ever had before. More confident, and more resolute in her certainty that not only did she need to get the hell out of Steelegate Prison, but it was her duty to guarantee that the fiends who fed on her and her fellow inmates for their own pleasure needed to pay for their crimes.

In the meantime, however, she kept to herself. She moved down to the lower bunk. She re-read Yvonne's tawdry novella through again. This time, she found herself enjoying the cloyingly vague descriptions of the heroine's physical intimacies. It had been a long time since anyone had touched Lena in that way, and late at night, alone in her cell, she contemplated the fact that unless she did something drastic, there was a very real chance she would never feel the crush of a man's body atop hers again—a living man, that is.

Also, she'd begun carefully watching Helen and Greta and Big Hal from a distance. Dottie had told her about the fight in the shower, and had hinted at what precipitated it.

The three were definitely up to something: they likewise avoided interacting with the other women, always whispering amongst themselves. In whatever daily routine was happening, they'd always lag behind. They'd even stopped bullying the weaker girls for smokes or the homemade hooch that some made in their cells. Then one afternoon in the Laundry, Lena had seen Hallie standing lookout. She'd managed to peer through the narrow space between two of the washing machines to see that behind Hallie's bulk, the other two were scraping away at the wall behind one of the mammoth dryers.

They were planning a breakout, even as Lena herself was contemplating her own.

13.

Christmas Eve

THERE HAD BEEN A SMALL Nativity play earlier, with several of the female prisoners dressing up as Joseph, Mary, shepherds, cows, and the like. But now it was late, and the Commissary had emptied out. Only Greta remained—tasked with cleaning up. Instead of cleaning, however, she was quickly and quietly shoving leftover rolls into a crudely sewn shoulder bag, looking all around her to make sure she was alone. Her face still bore faint yellowed marks of the blows Yvonne had landed.

Her bag full, she turned around suddenly and found Lena standing right there.

"What the hell are you doing sneaking around like that?" Greta snarled at her.

Lena peeked at the rolls in her bag: "Well I'm not sneaking muffins..."

The two stared at each other for a long moment. Lena nodded to the other girl's bruised face.

"I'm glad Yvonne didn't go down without a fight."

Greta shoved past the smaller woman.

"We were just looking to put a scare in her for—for certain reasons... it just got out of hand."

Lena grabbed her arm: "Was it Helen who killed her, or was it you?"

"Neither. When we left she was alive."

"I don't believe you."

"I'm a murderer, why would I lie about it? She wasn't gonna win any beauty pageants, but she was alive..."

Her voice lowered.

"I guess—they must have got to her."

"You think that it makes a real difference to me, if you killed her or if you just served her up to them on a plate? Because it doesn't."

Greta pulled loose from Lena's grip: "I gotta go."

Lena grabbed for the sack this time: "You can't."

Greta yanked it violently free.

"You're lucky I've got somewhere I've gotta be."

"I don't know why I'm trying to help you, I should let you go down with the other two."

Greta was almost to the door, but paused.

"Let me—what are you talking about..?" she turned to see Lena staring at her from the dim.

"They know."

"Know what?"

Lena sighed: "We don't have time to do this dance... they know all about the tunnel in the Laundry."

Greta's hand flashed out, grabbing Lena by the throat.

"Who did you tell, you little rat!?"

But Lena smacked her wrist away with surprising force.

"No one, you dummy. They've known all along..."

"You're lying. If they know then why haven't they stopped us?"

Lena was growing frustrated: "Are you really this dense? They haven't stopped you because they WANT you to try it. To go down there in the dark where there's no one to hear your screams... think about it. The only thing that keeps any of us remotely safe is being all together, up here where people—normal people, are watching. You go down there, and you're in their world. They can do whatever they want to you, and then say you died from lack of air in the tunnel, or it collapsed, or whatever. You're doing exactly what they want."

She could see Greta thinking about what she'd said, for about three seconds. Then:

"I gotta go."

"You're playing their game..." Lena watched her push her way out the door.

"Have a nice life, sucker. What's left of it."

•　　•　　•

It was almost lights out, and the guard Wallace was doing his cell check, calling out the roll in a voice too high-pitched for a man of his size.

"Twenty-three, clear! Twenty-five, clear! Twenty-seven—""

He stopped as he saw the empty cell. It took half a moment for what he was looking at to register, then he spun on his heel and hurried off, blowing his whistle.

•　　•　　•

The Laundry was abandoned at this time of night—piles of sheets and clothes caught in between washing and drying cycles were stacked everywhere.

Above, sirens began to go off all over the place, and Greta, Hallie and finally Helen slowly emerged from their hiding places under the piles.

Hallie looked around as she disentangled herself from the wet mess: "I gotta admit: I never thought that'd work..."

Helen held a finger to her lips.

"Quiet. We're on a deadline. Let's move..."

Quickly, they tiptoed past rows of hanging sheets to the large industrial washer. Helen nodded to Hallie:

"Okay, honey—your turn to shine..."

Hallie nodded, put her shoulder to the huge machine, and heaved. At first nothing budged, and the other two women shared a worried glance. Then slowly, with a horrible scraping sound, the machine started to shift. First an inch, then two.

Greta winced at the noise.

76

"They're gonna hear that!"

But Helen was tensed and ready: "Just a few more inches... c'mon, big girl..."

Behind the washer, a rough hole began to be visible. It had been crudely cut into the wall, opening into a cavernous darkness beyond.

Hallie shoved at the heavy steel contraption with all her might: one foot now, almost two—until suddenly with a *crack*, one of the iron feet of the machine snapped. The entire mighty weight of it slammed down on one corner with a BANG, the steel digging into the stone floor. All three women jumped back.

"What—?"

Hallie was already putting her shoulder back into it.

"Hurry up!" Greta hissed. Hallie shoved again. Hard. But after several tries, she was sweating and winded—she couldn't move it any more.

"I—can't... it's stuck now." She gasped.

Somewhere above them a light began to shine. They could hear shouting and running footsteps coming closer.

"How'd they know where we were?" Hallie asked.

"That little rat Lena! I shoulda shut her up when I had the chance." Greta picked up a heavy clothes rod, getting ready.

But Helen was peering into the narrow crevice revealed in the wall.

Greta turned: "You think we can fit?"

Helen was already pushing through the opening, squeezing her narrow frame through the space between the washer and the wall, barely able to make it. Once through, she poked her head back.

"C'mon!"

Hallie watched as in dismay as without another utterance, Greta shoved herself through the hole after Helen. The guards were getting closer.

"Guys?" She kneeled down to look at Helen and Greta on the other side. "I can't—there ain't no way I can make it through..."

Helen reached out a hand to lay on the big girl's shoulder.

"I know. Sorry, Hallie..." She turned and vanished.

Hallie's voice broke into a wail: "No wait! You can't leave me! They'll put me in the Hole for a year! You gotta help me move this!" She put her

77

back into it, shoving for all she was worth as the guards' flashes found her from above.

A male voice shouted: "There they are!" and boots clanked down the rickety steps.

Hallie kept pushing: "Please... help!"

Greta lingered behind at the opening for just for a second, staring at her. "Sorry... fatty."

And she was gone, too.

Hallie turned and the guards swarmed over all her, beating her with their nightsticks. She managed to smash a few of them in the process, crying with grief at her friends' betrayal the whole time.

"Lousy, miserable, lying——- I'LL SHOW YOU! You little men think you're tough?"

She seized one of the guards' batons and threw the man attached to it into the wall, turning and bashing another with it.

"You think I'm afraid? I'll show you something to be afraid of!"

She fought and kicked, bit and punched—but the guards were too many, and she finally went down under a pile of them.

•   •   •

In the dank cave beyond, Helen and Greta paused a second, listening to the sounds of the struggle—and for pursuers.

"I don't hear anyone coming... looks like they've got their hands full for the moment."

Greta fumbled in her bag, finally pulling out an old lantern she'd managed to purloin for the escape.

"Guess the big dummy was worth bringing in on this after all."

Helen suddenly turned and grabbed her, slamming her against the wall and nearly making her drop the precious lamp.

"Hey!"

Helen glared at her: "Maybe... and maybe I coulda done better than you."

A tense moment passed between the two, then she turned and hurried down the tunnel.

"C'mon. They'll be coming before long."

Greta's eyes scanned the dark tunnel behind them, searching it for signs of movement, seeing nothing, and she hurried after her.

•   •   •

Two of the larger-framed guards were sitting on top of Big Hallie in order to hold her down, but her struggles were still so furious that the other guards surrounding her were watching the handcuffs holding her thick wrists together with some concern.

"You're pansies, all of ya! Buncha brave strong men who gotta gang up on a girl to get her down... I get outta these cuffs and I'll show you buncha mama's boys some hurtin', you—"

She abruptly shut up as a pair of shiny wing tip shoes stepped into her line of sight. Her red-rimmed eyes tilted up as far as they were able, to see Warden Skelly staring down at her with a look of undisguised amusement on his pale face. The surrounding guards parted ranks and Wardens Oberlun, Smithfield and Tolifson came up behind him.

Warden Skelly slowly bent over at the waist until his face was very near Hallie's.

"Well, then... we seem to have discovered a bit of misbehavior, here, haven't we?"

The human guards looked at each other and smiled a bit nervously, as though afraid of what they might be about to see.

Warden Skelly glanced up at the hole in the wall, peering into the tunnel beyond.

"Hmmm... We're certainly going to have to put on our thinking caps to decide an appropriate punishment for this..."

Reginald the guard spoke up nervously: "Sir, the other two. They made it into the tunnels. Shouldn't we—?"

"Thank you, Reginald, that will be all for now. Would you and your fellows be so kind as to take our sizable miscreant here to Solitary Confinement, please?"

"Yes, but shouldn't we—?"

Warden Skelly's head cocked just the slightest bit and the guard knew he'd crossed an invisible line. A visceral chill hung suspended in the air.

"That. Will. Be. All." The Warden's voice remained soft but the steel in it was unmistakable. Reginald looked as if he'd just been slapped. He nodded to the others and they dragged Hallie to her feet with some difficulty, leading her out without another word spoken.

As she trudged up the steps, Hallie's eyes stayed on the Wardens standing in front of the escape tunnel until the last moment. Then she was out the door.

Alone finally, the Wardens all leaned forward in eerie unison, peeking through the opening, utilizing senses that were far keener than those of normal humans.

Warden Smithfield was the first to speak:

"They've not made it far."

Warden Skelly nodded. "Yes. Easily caught up to... But who to send after?"

He leaned back to survey his fellow Wardens present. All were quite obviously eager to be picked for this task. Considering carefully, he finally nodded to Oberlun and Tolifson. The two chosen Wardens nodded back, and were off after the escapees without a sound, disappearing into the caves.

Warden Smithfield watched them go in obvious disappointment.

"You never pick me..."

"Now, now, Warden... that's not true."

He leaned close enough to whisper: "I believe there's a generously-portioned treat waiting for you in the Solitary cell."

The shorter Warden's eerie eyes lit up at that. He gave Warden Skelly a slight bow, and then hurried off up the steps.

As Warden Skelly watched him go, calling after him.

"Remember to pace yourself, Warden... you know what happens when you eat too quickly."

• • •

Lena rose up from the lower bunk as she heard several pairs of feet coming down the corridor. She looked out through the window just in time to see Big Hallie being led towards the Hole by the small squadron of guards.

As they passed by, Hallie suddenly stopped, making two guards run into her from behind. The big woman turned to stare at Lena, and Lena knew she was in trouble.

Without warning and with a speed belying her formidable girth, Hallie rushed the door to Lena's cell, ramming it with her body and making it shudder, the impact knocking Lena back onto the floor.

Hallie's face squeezed into the small frame, as the Guards vainly struggled to pull her back.

"You little rat! You sold us out! "

Lena couldn't quite make her voice work right.

"No... no, it wasn't me, I swear! I tried to—""

"Bull! I know it was you! You better hope they finish me off down there, because if I make it out the first thing I'm doing is coming for you, you hear me?!"

The guards finally managed to peel her away, and hauled her down the hall, kicking and screaming the whole way. Her screams drifted back even as she was led off:

"You get that straight, I'm coming back for you! And I won't stop until I have your skin for a bedsheet, you hear me you little traitor? You hear me?"

Finally the door to the block slammed shut and Hallie was gone. Lena breathed a sigh of relief, sitting back down on her bunk. But slowly, she become aware of a growing sound of voices chanting, repeating a single word over and over, gradually growing in volume:

"Rat... rat... rat... rat... rat... Rat... rat... rat... rat... rat..."

The voices were coming from the other cells on the block. The walls echoed with their chant.

"Rat... rat... rat... rat... rat... Rat... rat... rat... rat... rat..."

One level up, in her own cell, Dottie was chanting along with the others, smiling as she did.

"Rat... rat... rat..."

"No! No, I didn't! It was THEM! They knew! I didn't tell ANYONE!" Lena yelled out of her cell.

But the chanting continued, unnerving her. She retreated back to her bunk, crawling into it, covering her ears with the thin pillow.

"Rat... rat... rat... rat... rat... Rat... rat... rat... rat... rat..."

14.

THE HOLE.

Hallie stood in the black, her back to the corner in the small cell, waiting. Her lungs took in big gulps of stale air as she got ready. She'd been here long enough to know what was coming for her in the dark. And she knew they'd be coming for her soon.

She heard the heavy iron door creak open, then slam shut again. She dug her heels in for traction, and got ready.

"You know I'm not going without a fight..."

From the darkness came the sibilant hiss of Warden Smithfield's voice:

"Oh... I'm most certainly counting on it..."

In the dim, Hallie saw the merest hint of a shadow moving silently against the moldy wall. Her eyes shifted left and right, trying to sense where her visitor was, and then in a shadowy blur he was on her, long fingers grasping her and razor teeth ripping at the flesh of her neck. Hallie screamed, grabbing hold of her attacker and hurtling him against the far wall with every ounce of her considerable strength.

The Warden was on his feet again in an instant, eyes a-glitter, circling his intended prey.

"Oh, but this is going to be enjoyable..." the ghoul smiled. Hallie could see her own blood glinting off his chin, and her hand went to her throat. It came away wet. She struggled for breath now—his initial attack had already taken a lot out of her. She was fighting to stay defiant against the panic that now swelled over her.

"Come at me again, and I swear I will make a slippery end of you."

Again his voice filtered from the darkness: "My dear, foolish girl... what your small minds fail to understand is that this is the very difference between your kind, and ours... we have no end."

In a blur, Smithfield catapulted behind the big woman, bouncing off the walls on all fours like an ape, and came crashing into her from behind with terrifying force.

Hallie's front smashed into the wall, as Smithfield's teeth once again sank into the pulsating arteries of her neck with a crunch of rending tissue and muscle. She hollered in pain. Then in an instant he was gone again, even as she swung a heavy haymaker at where he'd just been.

"Slow and clumsy, large lady... you're getting weaker."

Smithfield lunged again, but Hallie managed to catch him by his throat, holding him at bay.

"Fast enough to catch you, you little freak."

She tightened her grip, smiling with pleasure as she choked this thing that had come to kill her. Her friends had left her. She was never going to get out of this room—but she took pleasure in the knowledge that neither would he.

After a moment, though, her smile faded. The creature was grinning ghoulishly at her. Slowly his hand reached up and grasped her wrist, a sharp thumbnail pressing into her flesh—bending it further and further, until finally she cried out and let go, sinking to her knees.

"Silly girl. You cannot throttle what doesn't breathe..."

He yanked her arm out straight, burying his teeth in it, spinning her around and around until finally he released her, licking her blood from his lips with pleasure.

Hallie stumbled a step, rebounding off the far wall; she was fighting to keep her limbs working now. "Hope you brought your appetite..." she said through gritted teeth. "I got a lot of blood... this is gonna take you a good long a while."

"I'd be disappointed if it didn't..."

She caught just a glimpse of a moving shape in the black, and summoning the last molecule of her remaining strength, Hallie charged at it—only to feel herself pass through a swath of black raiment, before stumbling and crashing into the base of the cell's door. In an instant the thing was right on top of her, pinning her face to the floor, whispering in her ear.

"Poor, sad, Hallicent Lydecker... always the outcast... laughed at by the other girls at St. Mary's... Big Hallie, they called you, didn't they?"

She growled: "Shut up..."

"Big Hallie... ever the pariah... not like the other girls... Big Hallie with the one friend that didn't laugh... What was her name?"

"Shut up! You don't say her name!"

"But never meant to last: no one to cry to over a broken heart... no real friends... not then, not now... just more to betray you... in the end always back to being alone... abandoned... like now..."

His words hurt her at her core, but a part of her still reached deep down and found her anger again—her pride.

"Do it then... make the whole world go away, I don't give a rat's ass anymore... but just so you know... you may kill me..." she turned her head just enough to get a look at him: "But you'll still be an ugly son of a bitch."

Warden Smithfield didn't laugh at that. His face contorted into an animal-like snarl, and then he chomped down on her throat. Hallie cried out in agony as his teeth tore her skin and pierced her veins with a white-hot sting. She heard the churning of her own blood in her ears, then she heard nothing at all.

• • •

Warden Skelly stood staring with interest out the tall windows at an approaching storm front. Behind him, the door opened and closed again, and tentative footsteps approached. Human fear had a biting, sour smell to Skelly's nostrils—like fruit gone bad. He didn't have to turn to know it was Stephens standing there, holding his hat in his hands.

"You... you wanted to see me, Warden?"

Warden Skelly stared at the storm.

"Such an amazing display, isn't it, Mr. Stephens? Nature at its most primal. The elements of life and death clashing like some atmospheric chess match..."

Stephens didn't know what to say to that.

"Um.. Yeah. Okay, I guess."

"Many people fear rainstorms, I'm told. But I think it's more the thunder than the lightning that frightens them... the loud crash that follows the flash... sometimes long after. It's the expectation of the inevitable that scares your kind."

Stephens shifted more. "Maybe..."

The Warden finally turned and walked casually towards Stephens, who nevertheless stiffened. The rank odor increased.

"Which is ridiculous, of course... after all, thunder never hurt a soul. Sadly typical. People are always afraid of that which they can't see."

He came around behind him. Wardens Tolifson and Oberlun had emerged out of the shadows now, approaching slowly. Stephens was sweating profusely now. The reek was nearly intolerable.

Skelly stopped.

"Now. Let's talk a bit about your relationship with our inmate Dottie Carmichael."

• • •

The cave was dark and damp, covered in odd-colored molds and lichens. Helen and Greta stumbled down a steep slippery incline, splashing into a few inches of slowly moving water. Helen held the old oil lamp, which threw only a pale glow to lead their way.

"Hurry it up, they'll be coming any minute."

Greta checked behind them: "Are you sure you know we're going the right way?"

"Old Hazel made me memorize all the landmarks before she kicked the bucket... I haven't forgotten."

As they moved forward through a narrow crack between rocky walls, several rats scurried past their feet, startled by the flickering light, causing

Greta to squeal in surprise.

Helen stared at her.

"Really? Come on."

They headed on. As the two women disappeared into the dark caverns beyond, the light from the lantern died, and the crevice grew dark again. At the far periphery of its glow, several shadows followed.

•   •   •

It was past sunset when when Dr. Johanna Mears was finally able to finish updating the charts for the State Medical Examiner. She grabbed her coat and switched off the lights, making sure as always that the key to the clinic was in her hand before the door closed and locked behind her.

There was a lot of commotion tonight, with teams of guards searching every nook and crevice of the prison for the missing girls. But even with all that ruckus, she could still hear the eerie familiar echo of her heels clacking back at her as she hurried across the walkway, then down the stairwell to the exterior door. Johanna tried to leave the prison before dusk whenever possible. In the four years she'd been here, none of the Wardens had ever so much as implied any kind of threat towards her, but she'd seen too much of the aftermath of their appetites to ever feel anything resembling safety so long as she was within their domain—and Steelgate was, without question, utterly and completely their domain.

She was confronted with a blinding flashlight beam in the face when she exited the prison building. Recognizing her, the guard holding the electric torch moved on his way without a word. Mears watched him playing its beam all along the wall, up and down, as she made her way across the small side courtyard towards the tiny lot where she parked along with the prison's guards and assorted maintenance staff.

She was almost to her Hudson when she sensed someone behind her. In her time at Steelgate she'd learned to trust the spidery feeling the Wardens always evoked when they were close at hand.

She turned, and there was Warden Skelly, standing very near. He smiled down at Dr. Mears: "Lots of commotion tonight," his slippery whisper voice never ceased to unnerve her.

"I heard there's two of them?"

The Warden nodded.

"They found a way into the caves, via the Laundry. Some of my peers are... well, it won't be very long."

"Did you... do you need me to stay? In case either of them are—?" she asked tentatively. Somewhere inside, Mears realized with shame that she was hoping neither girl would come back needing her help. She was tired. She wanted to leave this hideous place behind for a few hours—to see her husband, to hold her children.

Skelly shook his head: "Very kind of you to offer, Doctor, but I wouldn't think so. These two particular inmates... well let's say I expect them to put up quite a fight."

"Very well, then." She turned to put her key in the door, when his voice froze her:.

"One more thing, if you please, Doctor."

She turned. He was still smiling. That damned smile.

"I had a call today. From the State Prison Board."

"I'm sorry..." she wondered what he was getting at. What this had to do with anything. "A call about... me?"

"Yes. In fact I had a long conversation with Mr. Pollock. He's the Superintendent for prisons in our area, I believe you might have met him?

"Yes..." her mind was racing. "Yes, we had a nice chat last time he was here with the—those ladies whose organization I can never remember."

"*Ladies' Benevolent Reformation Society*. An awkward title, I have to agree. Mr. Pollock and I spoke at some length about you, Doctor. And your... status here."

"My status?"

"He seems to think your skills are being wasted at Steelegate. He called to inform me that he's putting in for a transfer for you."

The word hit her like a physical blow.

"Transfer..."

He was still grinning: "Yes. Upstate, I believe, to one of the larger facilities. The paperwork is already in progress; I imagine we'll have an official letter for you before week's end. But I thought I'd give you the good news in person."

"Yes..." her mind was racing. "Thanks so much—it's very kind of you, Warden."

"We'll certainly miss you here, Doctor. But wise minds will prevail. Now if you'll excuse me: this situation needs attending to."

"Of course." She managed to say, and the Warden turned on his heel and within a few long strides was around the corner of the building, speaking to several senior guards. Johanna kept her feet planted on the ground until he was out of sight, then her hand grasped the hood of the car for support.

A transfer. It was all she could have hoped for—a chance to get away from this abattoir of a jail, away from these fiends. Free to return to something resembling a normal life. To never have her children exposed to the horrors she witnessed here daily. It was a gift.

It was also, most likely, a death sentence.

15.

Christmas Day

THERE HAD BEEN A CHURCH service earlier, and now the Commissary was crowded for a special Holiday lunch, but Lena sat eating all by herself. Between bites of cold, rubbery turkey and watery mashed potatoes, she caught glimpses of the other women giving her dark looks from the other tables. Not just one, or a small group: she was getting them from all around. It probably wasn't even half of the women there, but it felt like all of them were boring holes in her back with their accusing eyes. Big Hallie's words had had their intended effect. She was a rat, as far as most of her fellow prisoners were concerned. And a rat's life wasn't worth much.

She was ankle-deep in these dark thoughts when she sensed someone was standing impatiently next to her. She looked up to see a rotund guard named Francis standing over her.

"Cole. Doc wants to see ya after you're done eatin'."

"About what?"

"Funny, she musta forgot to tell me. Or maybe I forgot to ask because I don't care, I can't remember..."

He tossed a wooden block with a looped string onto the table in front of Lena, and walked away. Lena looked around at the dozens of pairs of venom-drenched eyes staring at her. After a moment she pushed her food away, picked up the pass and walked out of the cafeteria, her head down. She didn't have to look to know that the glares followed her as she went.

●　　●　　●

The clinic was dim and deserted. Lena's knuckles gave a soft rap on the door, which was ajar. When there was no answer, she cautiously entered.

"Hello? Doc? Anyone here?"

The room was empty and silent. The rays of the late afternoon sun shone in through its high windows to create bright squares on the cement floor. Lena stepped up onto the rug that covered much of the small office section. Funny, she thought, how you take little things like a rug for granted, until you find yourself in a place where they're all but absent. She was enjoying the feel of the soft pile under her heels, when a voice behind her spoke, startling her:

"That was fast."

Lena jumped and turned. Dr. Mears was coming towards her through the rays of light, holding a wicked-looking bone saw, the teeth of which glinted in the shine.

Lena made an effort to compose herself: "Yeah, well, I thought maybe I'd stop on the way and chat with my friends, but then I remembered: I don't have any left alive."

The Doctor halted a few steps away now.

"I'm your friend, Lena. You don't think I'm your friend?"

Lena looked the medical woman in the eyes.

"Friends help each other out... last we talked, you didn't seem too anxious to help me."

"Fair enough."

She walked past Lena, headed towards the operating corner of the Infirmary.

"Come on. I may have found a way to convince you otherwise..."

After a moment's hesitation, Lena followed her. They passed glass cabinets filled with jars and gleaming medical tools, and a row of wall vaults for storing cadavers, before finally coming to two operating tables pushed together under a glaringly bright light. Lena paused:

On the tables lay a hulking large body under a sheet. The Doctor pulled back the fabric to reveal Hallie's nude pallid body.

"They brought her in this morning... she didn't even make it a single night down in the Hole."

Lena orbited around the large corpse, spotting entire chunks of flesh that had been torn from Hallie's neck.

"They told me jailbreakers would meet a quick end... they weren't lying."

"Of course they weren't. They can't afford to have anyone escape, can they? What if that person told someone? And what if that someone believed them, even enough to investigate what goes on here? The only way they survive is through terror—scaring the prisoners, influencing the local politicians, intimidating the staff. It's a thin wire they walk, the Wardens. It would take so little to snap it... to end all this."

Lena looked up at the woman. "You said it was too dangerous. Your family—""

"I've been informed by the State Board that I'm being transferred to the Schroeder Sanatorium for Women up near Promontory Point in a few weeks."

Lena was confused: "But that's good, isn't it?"

"Do you really think they'll chance it?" the doctor asked. "That once away from here I won't talk to anyone about what I've seen? Do you think they'll trust that I've never spoken a word to my husband about the Wardens of Steelegate?"

She stared down at Hallie, lost in dread thought.

"No. I'll never make it to the Schroeder Sanatorium. There'll be a fire in the house. An accident on the road. No investigation, of course. Just an accident. Tragic, of course... but just an accident."

"Then you should get away now. You can do that. Just go home one night and never come back... take your family and get far, far away."

Mears shook her head.

"They'd find us... to the ends of the planet, they'd stop at nothing to find us and protect their nasty little secret."

She turned to Lena.

"Unless you get out—and do what you said you'd do... bring this place and its masters down."

The two women stared one another down in silence for a moment:

"How?"

The Doctor glanced down towards Hallie.

"I looked over her sheet this morning. She has no family. No next of kin. Tomorrow she'll be taken out to Potter's Field. It's about an hour away, not far from my house. There's an unmarked plot out there waiting for her."

Lena wasn't following the Doctor's logic.

"Okay..."

"She was a big girl."

"Yeah, she was."

"Big stomach cavity... A lot of space inside taken up with organs: heart, stomach, liver, lungs, intestines..."

Lena was starting to get it now. Her eyes went to the body.

"You can't be serious..."

"When an inmate dies, I'm required by law to remove those organs, weigh them and examine them for infectious diseases... after my examination the organs are replaced and the body sewn shut again for burial."

She was definitely getting it now.

"How much do those organs weigh?"

The doc shrugged: "Maybe not as much as a small woman, but not too much less. Not so much that anyone carrying her would notice the difference—not with her size."

Lena stared at Hallie's motionless body, deciding.

"When?"

"Tomorrow evening. Right after dinner. They're picking her up at eight. She'll be on a truck and out the gate before bed check. I'll write you another note to come see me: put on the log that you have a bladder infection and need regular shots."

"That simple?"

"I can only get you outside the walls... the rest will be up to you. Can you do it?"

Lena only took a moment to decide. She laid a small hand on at Hallie's thick wrist.

"This place will kill me one way or the other... Whether it's quick or slow... figure I might as well make it on my own terms, right?"

Mears looked up at the large clock on the wall: "You better get back to your cell."

She turned to go, then paused.

"Thank you, Doctor."

The Doctor nodded.

"Merry Christmas, Lena."

16.

LENA WALKED IN SILENCE BACK to her cell. She passed no one on the way. The entire prison was on lockdown, and a queer pall had fallen over it, rendering the place even quieter than normal.

She entered her cell and sat down on her bunk, still lost in thought. After a moment something made her look up at the still-open door.

Warden Skelly was there, staring at her with a bemused expression.

Lena reflexively stood up and lowered her eyes.

"Good evening, Warden."

Skelly stared at her a long moment before replying, cocking his head as if he was trying to figure something out. Lena could have sworn he was sniffing around at her scent. Then finally:

"It would seem you're having a little trouble fitting in, here, Miss Cole."

"Nothing... nothing I can't handle, sir."

"Nothing you feel the need to speak with me about? Or perhaps Doctor Mears has a more... sympathetic ear."

She stared at him, trying to figure out how much he knew. Had he already figured out the plan? Had he been listening? Or was he just fishing?

"I just have a... little problem with my plumbing. She's giving me shots."

His expression gave her nothing. "I see. These little problems do seem to abound around you."

He continued to stare at her. Lena shifted from one foot to the other in discomfort. The moment seemed to hang indefinitely.

95

"Sleep well, Miss Cole."

He turned and was gone without a sound. Lena let out a quiet sigh of relief—only to be startled when a guard slammed her door shut and locked it.

"Everyone in their cells for headcount."

The guards begin calling out the roll, as Lena's eyes stared at the spot where Skelly had stood a moment before. She knew that the chance she was taking was nothing less than life and death, but she was only now realizing that the odds of it ending with the latter were, indeed, far greater.

• • •

The rising sun struck a glancing blow to the façade of the keep, casting long shadows across its cracks and crevasses.

Lena stood in line, waiting her turn for the showers, hyper-aware of every movement around her—the other prisoners shifting impatiently, the guards strolling up and down the line with their billy clubs.

The line moved forward a few feet, and when it halted again, the girl behind her bumped into her, almost knocking her down. She recognized Dottie's voice:

"Move it, rat. I don't got all day..."

The girl behind Dottie smirked.

"Dont'cha know, Dottie? Rats don't like the water..."

The girl behind that girl—a blotchy-faced woman named Pearl—added her own two cents: "That's how my daddy used to take care of 'em.. Put 'em in a sack and drown 'em... best way to kill rats."

The guard strolling past gave Pearl a light rap with his club.

"No talkin' in the line! Pipe down, all of ya! Eyes front!"

They all turned back to face forward. As they took another step closer, Dottie leaned forward to whisper in Lena's ear.

"Can you swim, little rat?"

She was rewarded for her disobedience as the guard grabbed her by her hair and yanked her out of line, hauling her to the back.

"I told you once—back of the line, you!"

Glancing back, Lena could see Dottie mouth the word 'RAT' as she

96

was dragged to the rear.

•　　•　　•

There was a certain room near the top of the tower of the Administration Wing that was known to be off limits to everyone: prisoners of course, but also the guards, any visitors, even superintendents. Everyone. Its heavy double door was made of steel-reinforced timbers, and was secured from the inside by many locks and reinforcements.

Had anyone else but the Wardens ever been allowed inside, they would have found the décor inside surpassingly strange: tall ceilings supported by arching wooden buttresses soared dozens of feet above, but no windows allowed a view from this enviable vantage. No lamps or candles provided illumination. In fact no decoration of any kind adorned the room, and no furniture filled the space—none of course, but eight wooden boxes scattered in a seemingly random way around the wooden floor.

They were each of them more than six feet long, but narrow. All were made with extreme skill so their jointures met with incredible precision, and their lids fit snugly. Some lay near the corners of the stony walls, some near the center, but at odd angles. Only one leaned against a far wall, and was covered in dust from long disuse.

17.

THE YARD.

Lena was shuffling cautiously around in a circle with the other girls during the afternoon exercise time, keeping alert as she watched a dozen unfriendly faces in the crowd. Soon it would be time for her to go to the infirmary, and she was working hard to control her excitement as well as her fear.

As she walked, she felt a hand press something into hers.

Bonnie's voice whispered in her ear:

"They're coming for you. Right now."

Lena turned: "Who?"

But Bonnie was gone, melted back into the crowd of women. Before she could look at what she'd given her, raised voices caught her attention, and Lena looked over to see the guards having a heated discussion with several of the *LBFRS* ladies at the gate:

The guard named Northrop was arguing with the woman, who were refusing to budge:

"I'm sorry, ladies—without an appointment, I can't let you in."

Millicent Chandler tensed: "My dear dense man, you must understand this is an urgent issue. I must speak with Warden Skelly *immediately*."

Northrop shook his head: "Warden's otherwise occupied, so that just ain't gonna happen, lady."

"How dare you speak to her that way, you crude little creature!"

Marguerite Vanderbosh scolded.

"Yeah, you're breakin' my heart. Now you go on home, and you call the office, and make an appointment and get a pass, and we'll let you in. There's a way this works, see?"

Millicent Chandler turned on her heel.

"You have NOT heard the last of this, young man..."

As she was watching this all happen, Lena didn't hear Dottie as she come up from behind and grabbed her around the neck. More hands clutched at the hem of her dress, or wrapped around her ankles as she struggled. She tried to yell out, but a filthy rank rag was shoved in her mouth.

She could see, amidst the flurry of bodies, that she was being carried towards the doors to the basement, where Minnie was standing watch. She thrashed and kicked, trying to get free—but all the while she kept a tight grip on what Bonnie gave her.

Inside, Lena was dropped to the hard ground, and felt a foot strike her ribs painfully.

"Up. Walk. You know the way."

She did. She stood, and Dottie and Minnie shoved her towards the stairs leading down to the Hole.

•   •   •

It took them a while of walking to get there, but finally they filed down the narrow stone steps to the tiny hallway with its three steel doors, and Lena was shoved against the wall. Minnie blocked the stairs as Dottie and Pearl surrounded her.

"Maybe you haven't been here long enough to realize that the other girls in here are the only family you'll ever have, girl. What could possibly have made you betray them to those fiends?"

"I told you I didn't—" that earned her a sharp slap to the face from Dottie.

"I guess we shouldn't be surprised... after all, she did off her own kid."

Minnie shook her head. "You are some kind of crazy, lady."

"—and you're gonna learn what happens to squealers in here."

99

Pearl added.

She pulled a sharpened piece of broom handle from behind her back, and came at her.

"No, not yet!" Dottie whispered, but too late.

Lena's hand fumbled with what Bonnie gave her: a toothbrush with a honed edge on its handle.

As Pearl moved forward, stabbing clumsily at Lena with her stick, Lena managed to dodge it, and grabbed the other girl around the throat, putting her weapon against her jugular.

"Drop it," she muttered. "Please, I don't want to have to hurt you. But I swear I will."

The broom handle fell at their feet. Dottie and Minnie stared at them.

Lena's brain raced. She had to get out of here. She had to get up to the commissary so she could be sent to the Doctor. It was all so close to unraveling.

"Now both of you are going to back away... or the Wardens are gonna have to lap your friend's blood up off the floor."

Dottie nodded. "Go ahead. But you're not going anywhere. "

Pearl stared at her friend. "Dottie?"

"Sorry, Pearl. You should have waited for me to say."

She pulled out a crude pair of brass knuckles, their edges sharpened into jagged spikes.

"Dot, you can't let her kill Pearl." Minnie squeaked.

A voice came down to them from somewhere above: "Of course she can."

They all turned to look up the rough flight of stairs. Greta stood at the top. She was filthy, her clothes shredded, and half of her body was covered in dark, dried blood.

"Impossible..." Dottie whispered.

"See,' Greta said, "she has to let you all die down here in this pit. That's the plan. She doesn't have another choice, because—"

"Because she's the one that ratted you three out to the Wardens." Lena finished Greta's sentence.

Pearl and Minnie gave each other a look as Greta limped down the final stairs.

"The new girl's a smart one, you gotta give her that," she said.

"Dottie?" Pearl stared at her friend, then her face fell.

Millie snarled: "You rat. You aughta be ashamed of yourself."

Dottie looked at the women all around her, and she knew it was all over. With a shrug, she turned and punched Millie in the face with the knuckles, slashing her skin open. Millie screamed. Dark red blood went everywhere.

Pearl's elbow slammed into Lena's belly. The woman spun 'round and grabbed her by the throat, shoving her up against the stones.

Greta charged Dottie, who swung wildly with the knuckles and missed as Greta ducked, slamming her to the ground and grabbing her dangerous hand.

Lena and Pearl struggled, until Lena finally got her hand free, and managed to stab the woman in the side with the toothbrush. It went in several inches. Pearl screamed, and sank down to the ground.

Dottie and Greta rolled back and forth on the floor, locked in their struggle and bouncing back and forth off either wall. Finally Dottie managed to roll on top, and began pushing her bladed fist down towards Greta's throat. Greta was stronger, but gravity gave Dottie the advantage. The rusty metal was grazing the skin when there was a crack, and Dottie toppled over. Greta looked up to see Lena holding the broken end of the broom handle.

She helped her up.

"Why on earth did you come back?" she asked, and a haunted look passed over the tall woman's face:

All around them was dark, and shapes seemed to surround Greta and Helen. As they fled through the caverns, they became separated into two different passages.

Through a stalactite wall, Greta watched helplessly as Helen was torn to pieces by the Wardens, who then drained the parts of all their blood.

She ran. She fled as far into the deep as she could, her way illuminated by grotesque, glowing fungi, which clung to the walls. She could no longer hear them following. Finally the light faded into darkness, and she lost her footing, sliding down a steep incline to find herself lying prone in a vast cavern. Slowly she came to realize that the entire floor was covered with bones. The bones of animals. The bones of people. The bones of babies.

She clutched a hand over her mouth and screamed in silence.

Greta shook her head: "We never made it out..." She swayed a bit, lost in the hideous memory. The dinner bell rang up above, startling them both.

"Your breakout is tonight, isn't it?"

Lena could only nod.

Greta looked down at the girls on the floor.

"Then I guess you'd better go."

"What about them?"

"Leave these ladies to me."

Lena went up a few steps and paused.

"Hey..."

Greta didn't turn.

"Don't... just go."

Lena paused just a moment, then turned and ran up the steps. Once she was gone, Greta leaned down and grabbed Minnie, who was still moaning and holding her side, by the collar and began dragging her.

"C'mon, honey... time to make yourself useful."

●　　●　　●

Lena managed to dart into the Commissary just as Willie the guard was closing the door.

"Where you been? Almost missed out on dinner..."

"I, uh... sorry. Bathroom."

Willie just scowled. "Get in there."

He shoved her in and shut the door behind her.

There was no line for food this late, and within a few minutes Lena was sitting down with her tray of meatloaf and gravy. Yvonne had been right— the meatloaf was pretty good. But tonight Lena just picked at it. She had no real appetite. She caught herself repeatedly glancing up anxiously at the clock, then over to where her attackers normally sat.

Their seats were empty. As Lena glanced around, she could see guards whispering to one another. As she looked she spotted several Wardens moving towards the guards. They discussed something in hushed voices, casting suspicious glances all around, and Lena ducked down to stare at her dinner again, sticking a few forkfuls in her mouth. It might be the last meal she had in a while.

Within seconds her eyes went to the clock again. She couldn't help it. She was growing more and more anxious. Something had gone wrong. No one was coming to take her to the doctor. The incident with the other girls had likely thrown everything off. Now she saw several more of the Wardens had shown up, and the discussions with the guards were growing more intense. The other girls could see it as well, and everyone was whispering.

Lena eased her tray away. She was going to have to sneak out of the commissary to get to the clinic. She was watching all the staff, trying to pick her moment, when a heavy hand fell on her shoulder, making her start.

"You."

She'd been so focused on the clock she hadn't noticed the guard Halloway approaching until he was standing right next to her.

"Come on, you: Doc wants to see you right now."

Lena tried to disguise her sigh of relief as she stood and headed for the door.

Halloway, as was his custom, led her by the arm all the way to the infirmary. As they passed the door that led down towards Solitary, Lena tensed despite herself, and he tugged her along.

"No dawdling, come on."

They passed through the cellblock checkpoint, and came to the raised steel catwalk which led to the administration wing.

"You know, I know the way myself... I've gone here before alone."

"No prisoners on their own when we've got anyone unaccounted for. That's the rules." Halloway was always a stickler for the rules.

There was nothing more for Lena to say, but as they neared the end of the catwalk she saw someone coming from the other side, approaching. The harsh overhead light bounced off a pale, hairless head, and Lena realized it was Warden Smithfield.

Halloway pulled her to a stop as he approached:

"Evening, sir."

The Warden glanced up and down at Lena with unmistakable distaste.

"Where are we going with this one?"

"Infirmary. Doc says she needs her shots."

Smithfield leaned a fraction closer to Lena—he almost seemed to be sniffing her.

"And what exactly is your physical complaint, my dear?"

Lena hesitated a fraction of a second: "I—-- I don't know... she says something wrong with my... when I go to the bathroom."

The Warden wrinkled his nose in distaste.

"Disgusting... and trivial. Take her back to her cell until we find the others."

Halloway nodded a "Sir", and pulled Lena into an about face.

"C'mon, you."

Lena was panicking inside. As Halloway tugged at her arm she jerked him to a stop:

"She said—she said it might be... infectious."

The guard involuntarily let go her arm. Warden Smithfield stared at her for a long time. Lena shifted nervously under his unwinking gaze, but held her ground.

The Warden's mouth curled slightly when he finally spoke.

"Very well."

He nodded to the door behind him and Halloway escorted Lena past him.

As they reached the door and Halloway fumbled with his keys, Lena hazarded a glance back. Smithfield was still in the same position, watching them go. Then they were through the portal and the door swung shut and he was mercifully gone. But his lingering stare worried her.

As he hauled Lena into the infirmary, Halloway called out in a harsh whisper: "Doc? Hey, DOC?" and Doctor Mears emerged out of the shadows. She was wearing a bloody apron.

"Right here, Joseph, you don't have to whisper:—" she nodded behind her to the row of tables, on which lay several cadavers: "y—you won't be waking any of them up."

Halloway gave a shiver at the sight, forgetting what he was doing for a moment, then:

"They said you wanted this one for something, doc?"

"I did. Thank you." She nodded to Lena: "Over here, girl."

Lena followed the Doctor towards the examination area. When they got there, they both noticed Halloway still standing there.

"Thank you, Joseph... that'll be all."

"Oh, I gotta stay, Doc. Rules. She's gotta be accompanied by staff."

"Yes. And I'm one of the staff, Joseph. You can go, I'll take responsibility."

Halloway shuffled nervously, running through the rules in his head.

"No... see, they told me—"

"Joseph? Please remember that I'm in charge of the Medical Wing. Now I have to perform a pelvic exam on this girl, and for that we require privacy. She's entitled to that. Alright?"

He debated that, conflicted—but finally nodded.

"Okay. Call us if you need anything, Doc."

"Of course I will. Thank you for understanding."

He finally left, his boots scuffling as they went. Lena and Dr. Mears listened to them retreating back down the catwalk until they were inaudible, and both breathed a sigh of relief.

"I thought he wasn't gonna budge."

Mears smiled: "Well, I DO outrank him—he just needed to be reminded of it. Now hurry, we only have a few minutes before they'll be coming for the body."

She led the way back to where Hallie's body lay on the table. Lena was again struck by the woman's sheer size, and girth.

"How did—?"

"Took three guards to get her up on the table for me, and I'm pretty sure one of them has a hernia now."

"I bet."

"It'll be a tight fit. I'm afraid every inch counts. You're going to have to strip down as much as possible."

Lena watched silently as the Doctor went to work with a series of instruments from a table at hand: her scalpel effortlessly cut a vertical slit down her front, bisecting Hallie's torso from neck to groin. Next the doctor pulled out a foot-long saw with two vertical handles on either side. Its shining sharp teeth glistened.

"You may find this sound—well, just get ready."

In another second Mears was using the saw to cut through the bones of the ribcage, eliciting a grotesquely wet sound that was both a crunch and a crack.

Lena watched, unblinking at it. Mears saw her expression and nodded.

"You might just be able to do this."

The Doctor then inserted a long, horizontal tool with gears and a kind of handle on one end.

"This is called a rib spreader." And with that she cranked the handle, which had the effect of separating the two sides of Hallie's sternum apart with an awful popping sound. With some effort, she kept cranking, but her strength was sapping.

"This... is normally... difficult... but with someone... this large..."

Lena moved forward: "Here. Let me give you a hand."

She took hold of the handle below the Doctor's grip, and together they cranked it the rest of the way—Hallie's ribs cracked and splintered and a godawful smell arose from the body cavity. Lena fought the urge to gag.

"That's normal," Mears said. "Gases escaping and partially-digested food. It'll get better when we get it all out."

The rib spreader reached its maximum width.

"Okay, that's it. Far as it goes. Sorry, it's gonna be a tight squeeze."

As the doctor cleaned out the organs, slicing through tissue and scooping it onto a heavy scale nearby, Lena stared down at what lay before her. She'd expected blood and bone, but Hallie's insides were a frightening mix of colors and textures: purple organs and yellow layers of fat, green bile and brown meat. The charnel smell of it was indescribable.

"Last chance. You can go back to your cell and be safe."

Lena's eyes caught hers. "No, I really can't."

"You're sure about going through with this, then?"

"Yeah. I'm sure... are you?"

"Just do what you said you would."

Lena nodded, taking off her shoes and stripping off her linen dress and handing the bunch to Mears, who stuck them into a discard bin along with

Hallie's clothes. Now in just her slip, Lena began to climb up onto the table.

She stepped inside the body cavity, wincing at the squishy feel on her feet.

"She's... cold."

"I know. They get like that. Please, we have to hurry."

Lena worked her hips through the narrow gash, wiggling to get herself in under the ribs. She decided it would be better to curl up with her head pointed towards Hallie's hips—this way her legs could fit up under the sternum where her lungs and heart had been. It took some wiggling. There was viscous, coagulated blood everywhere.

A thought occurred to her: "Will I be able to breathe?"

"It's a loose stitch... it won't be pleasant, but you should have plenty of air... just remember:" she handed Lena a small scalpel.

"Do not lose that. When they load her off the truck, and into the preparation room, you should have a few minutes. That's your moment. If you don't get out then, they'll put her in her coffin and nail it shut. Then you're finished. They'll be no getting out after that. You'll be buried alive inside her in potter's field."

Lena stared up at the woman. "I'll manage."

In a moment Doctor Mears was unwinding the rib stretcher, and the hole began closing above Lena's face. Lena had to force down a moment of panic as it grew dark around her inside the body, but she managed to hold herself together. The body closed, Doctor Mears moved away a moment to get the needle and suture, and Lena was left with a moment to herself, to reflect on the sheer insanity of what she was doing—then the doctor was back.

"Okay, this is it. Good luck."

"You too."

"Keep your face down. I don't want to stick this through your nose by mistake."

"Right."

Doctor Mears sewed Hallie's stomach up with a quick and practiced stitch. Lena counted thirteen sutures from the center of Hallie's chest to the top of her pubis. But as the doctor was almost done, Lena heard a soft knocking on the clinic's door. She froze.

Mears' voice gave out a creaky "Enter..." and then Lena could hear her give out a barely audible gasp.

"Ah, Doctor... I'm glad I found you still here..." Warden Skelly's voice echoed.

18.

DR. MEARS FOUGHT TO QUELL the panic rising inside her, and returned to calmly stitching: "Yes... I was just finishing up for the evening, actually. Getting this one ready to go out tonight. Can I help with anything, Warden? Is this about Guard Halloway? Because—"

Warden Skelly moved towards them without sound of footfall, giving no hint as to whether he suspected anything odd.

"Joseph? No, not at all."

The tall creature came to stand next to the doctor—the proximity to the body obviously did not bother him the way it would an ordinary person.

"I merely wanted to offer you my personal congratulations regarding your imminent transfer, Doctor... You must be very excited."

She was caught off-guard by that: "I am, thank you—very nice of you to take the trouble, Warden. The Schroeder should be a... rewarding challenge... managing a small medical staff... more patients."

"And so close to the water. I'm sure your young ones will enjoy it immensely..."

Mears visibly tensed at the mention of her children. Struggling to maintain her composure, she finished closing the body and pulled the sheet overtop.

Lena was now plunged into near-total darkness. She exerted all her willpower towards keep her breathing silent and her heart from pounding.

Mears rallied: "Yes. Well, they're sad to leave their school friends, but

I'm sure you're right: they'll enjoy the... water."

She glanced up to see Warden Skelly staring down at her. He held the gaze for a long, uncomfortable silent moment.

"Is anything... wrong, Doctor?"

"No... no, it's just these—unaccounted for prisoners Joseph mentioned... makes me a bit nervous, is all."

"Well, you may relax, we discovered them down in the solitary wing a few minutes ago."

Lena tensed.

"Oh. Really..?" Mears asked.

"Yes... up to some kind of mischief-making, I'm sure, that went awry. They had managed to lock themselves *inside* the cell, if you can believe it. "

"These girls... one wonders what goes through their heads."

The tall creatures smiled: "One does. The guards are fetching the spare key now from my office. I—"

Skelly paused a moment, as if hearing something that didn't make sense. His head cocked the slightest bit.

"Warden?"

But instead of answering, the Warden reached out, lightly touching Hallie's neck, subtly feeling for the pulse he thought he'd heard a moment ago.

"Poor, misunderstood creature... never meant to have a place in this world..."

Lena closed her eyes, willing her heart to be silent, holding her breath until her lungs burned.

"I'm sorry, Warden? But I was hoping to get home before..."

Skelly seemed to snap out of it—like the moment never happened. "Indeed... Well, I'll not keep you overlong, Doctor; you must be anxious to get home to your charming family."

"Yes. Thank you, Warden."

He turned to go, and Lena breathed a silent sigh of relief.

The doctor's body tensed again as Warden Skelly paused at the door, slowly turning and giving her a small smile, then the doors closed again and he was gone.

The Doctor grabbed a table for support, almost collapsing—shaking, catching her breath. In a flash she grabbed up a pair of scissors, going to the body.

"He knows... he knows, I can tell he knows..." Her shaking hands fumbled with the shears, trying to get at the sutures. "We can't... he knows, he knows..."

Lena pushed her fingers against the sewn-up opening, popping it between the sutures and grabbing at the Doctor's wrist.

"Doc, stop! It's done. It's too late."

"No. I can make it right... my family, my kids..."

Lena's eye peered through the slit in Hallie's flesh.

"Do you think he cares if you do this thing or if you were just planning to do it? You think that'll change what he does?"

Mears stopped at that, the words striking home.

She jumped again when the infirmary doors banged open. But instead of the Warden it was two grungy men in overalls, wheeling a creaking gurney.

"Hey, Doctor, we're here for the biggun'..."

He nodded to Hallie's cadaver. Mears looked down as Lena snatched her hand back in. There was a moment when Lena wasn't sure what she would do. Finally the doctor answered mechanically: "Of course. I was just... leaving."

The two men went about moving the heavy body to their conveyance as Mears numbly picked up her coat, gloves and purse.

"I have to go home now... my husband and children will be wanting their supper..."

The older gravedigger, a thick set man named Muskie, grinned at her through silver teeth: "Alright, Doc... you say hi to those little dumplings for us, will ya?"

"Of course I will... thank you."

She teetered out of the room, stumbling once just a bit. "Please turn out the lights when you leave, thank you..."

Once she was gone, the two men look at each other and snickered—the younger one, Clifford, mimicking taking a stiff belt of booze and nodding the way she went.

Muskie cracked his thick knuckles: "Alright, now, let's get this done...

and one, two, three HEAVE!"

With a grunt they transferred Hallie—and Lena inside—onto the gurney. She landed with a bone-shuddering thud that shook Lena's molars.

"Lord, if she ain't a whale..."

"My back's gonna be barkin' tomorrow, I tell ya that..." Muskie agreed.

He threw a rough burlap blanket over Hallie, and they started to roll her out.

Inside, Lena bounced around as they rolled out towards the exit, listing to the men talk.

"Hard to believe anyone ever picked a fight with this one..."

"Maybe she had two lovers..."

"What, like one for the top, one for the bottom?"

They both cracked up at that as they wheeled their charge out.

•　　•　　•

The heavy front door swung onerously open, and Muskie, Clifford, Hallie and Lena rolled out of the prison proper. The two men negotiated the heavily laden stretcher onto the raised platform, against which an older model truck was parked. A guard standing next to the truck holding a clipboard and paperwork nodded as they approach him.

"Gentlemen..."

Muskie looked around in mock panic: "Where?"

The gravediggers both burst into laughter, but the guard just stared at them without a hint of amusement.

"Right, you two outta be in Vaudeville with that bit. Alright, let me check, here..."

He lifted the burlap, checking Hallie's face with a hand torch against the picture on her prison card.

He squatted down and peered under the gurney for stowaways.

"Any free riders under there, Clancy?"

Clancy stood up again, straightening his suit with dignity: "I'm required to check, you two knuckleheads know that... be my hiney *and* your'n if one of the girls got out through us... you wanna find out what kinda hell they rain down on thems that fall down on their duty around here?"

He nodded up to the windows. The gravediggers followed his gaze, and they all realized that one of the Wardens stood in the window above, staring down at them.

"Oh, Lord, almighty..." Clifford whispered.

"We 'bout done here, Pal?"

"Yeah. Let's get you two commodians moving." The guard shoved his clipboard at Muskie and Muskie marked it with an X.

 "Alright, take her on outta here."

As they wheeled the body into the truck he patted the heavy body.

"Bye now, Hallie..."

Lena could now feel herself and Hallie being lifted into the back of the truck.

"Tie her down, we don't want her rolling back and forth on those curves up ahead... damn near tip us over, won't she?" The two men finished their task and Lena heard the rear doors shut on her, then came the sound of the front bench springs squeaking as the men climbed into the cabin.

From above, Skelly and several other Wardens watched with acute interest as the truck pulled out of the gate and drove away. Then they looked at each other, and nodded.

19.

THE TRUCK RUMBLED ALONG THE country road, its old tires finding every pothole.

Inside her prison of flesh and bone, Lena braced herself against every harsh bump. Barely able to move her arms, she tried in vain to wipe away a reeking, unidentifiable fluid that had started oozing down onto her face. In doing so, she realized she'd lost hold of the scalpel the Doctor gave her— she reached around blindly for it and finally found it laying down low in the cavity, near Hallie's spine: getting hold if it again she breathed a little sigh of relief, and tucked it into the waistband of her underwear.

Up front, the two gravediggers stared through the cracked windshield ahead at the road.

"I'll tell ya... I don't ever mind leaving that place..."

"Well of course ya don't, dummy... it's a prison after all."

"That ain't what I'm talking about and you know it, Muskie."

Muskie drove on for a bit, only casting his partner a brief sideways glance.

"I thought we had us an understanding, Cliff... that we weren't gonna talk about none of that out loud..."

Clifford shook his head: "Come on, cuz, we're two miles away in the middle of nowhere with only a stiff in the back—"

If either had looked back into the rear of the truck at that moment, they might have caught, almost invisible amongst the shadows, a subtle movement at the foot of the body: a shape lurking in the dark.

"—who's gonna hear us?"

•   •   •

Warden Smithfield led the way down the stairs to the Solitary Wing. Several guards marched behind him, riot sticks gripped tightly in their clenched hands.

"There now, hold on ladies. We'll be in to fetch you in just a moment..."

In the dimness inside the cell, the two girls struggled, mumbling inarticulately as the key rattled in the lock and the door suddenly opened, allowing light to spill over the cell and the half-dozen gasoline cans lined against its wall. It also reflected off of the large pool of gas covering the floor.

As the heavy metal door swung open, it pulled a road flare, which was wired to the inside, dragging it along the stone and sparking it to life.

Smithfield's uncanny eyes only had a moment to widen in the growing yellow light, before the blast immolated everyone in the hallway.

Greta stood at the top of the stairs looking down with satisfaction, closing her eyes as the fireball rose up towards her.

The great ball of flame erupted out the side of the prison edifice, making a hole large enough to drive a truck through, and casting bricks and stone a thousand feet down to the valley below as inmates throughout the prison cheered.

•   •   •

The lonely building was old and decrepit. It had housed a blacksmith's forge in times long past, so part of it was built of stone. This well-served its current purpose, since the stone walls helped insulate it from the heat, thus slowing the decomposition of the bodies it frequently held before their internment.

The morgue truck was parked near a ramp that led up to a large sliding door. Nearby were stacks of cheap lumber—tar pine and knotted spruce—building materials for the dead.

The two men groaned as they pushed the heavy gurney carrying Hallie up the wooden ramp and into the preparation room.

"Lord!"

Muskie grunted in reply: "Don't... talk... just... PUSH!"

Inside, the walls were lined with crudely built coffins. In the light of a single flickering bare bulb, they cast long oblong shadows.

But inside her damp, reeking hideout, Lena could see none of this.

Coming to a halt in the center of the preparation room, Muskie and Clifford looked at each other's sweaty faces.

"Supper?" Clifford asked.

"Supper." The other replied.

They both turned and headed back to the truck, leaving Hallie's body lying under its rough sheet. It lay still and silent on the gurney for quite a few moments, before the stomach began to slowly distend.

In the pitch black, Lena slowly negotiated herself into an upright-facing position before carefully reaching down and pulling the scalpel from her waistband.

The point of the scalpel emerged through the slit in Hallie's stomach, sliding down to cut the first of the coarse catgut sutures.

Working by feel, Lena negotiated the blade downward, opening up the cavity stitch by stitch. She knew she had to hurry, but she also knew everything depended on her being cautious in this moment. The flesh above her head was parted a few inches now, and she could better see what she was doing. But as she was almost halfway through opening Dr. Mears' original incision, she found herself having to bend awkwardly in the middle to reach, and suddenly her hand unexpectedly punched right through the outer belly wall, and she lost her grip on the scalpel. There was an empty second, and then she heard it tinkling onto the stone floor below. Lena froze, waiting, listening for sounds of the gravediggers coming to see what the noise was. She fought down the welling panic, forcing her breathing to remain quiet.

Nobody came. Outside, Muskie and Clifford were eating paper-wrapped sandwiches, taking slugs from a thermos of spiked coffee.

This has already taken too long, Lena was thinking to herself. With nerveless fingers she reached up and felt for the next stitch, tugging on it.

Each suture was tied off on its own, so even though she'd cut through the first several, it wouldn't come free. Lena reached a cautious hand through the opening to try tugging at it from the other side, but with no more luck. The hole was only ten inches. She couldn't squeeze out yet. The window to escape was quickly closing.

She pulled her arm back in and scrunched down as far as she could inside the slippery cavity. Pressing her face against the gory inside wall, she managed to get the thread between her teeth and bit down on it, tearing at its sinewy fibers until it finally broke.

She dug into it now, gnawing furiously at the remaining stitches. As they started to come loose, she gripped the fleshy sides of the opening, tearing Hallie's flesh as she fought to free herself.

Finally Lena had the gash open, and she thrust her head out of the body. The air inside the makeshift morgue was stale and reeked of wood rot and bodily decay, but she happily sucked it in after her confinement. She worked her arms free one by one, having to bend over to yank free the last two sutures, and then—with some effort—she pulled her lower half out until, covered in blood and unnamable body fluids like some adult-born cesarean, she was finally free of the cadaver.

Free, but not out of trouble.

Forced to hold the cramped position so long, her legs had fallen asleep. Lena tumbled off the gurney and onto the floor with a thud that shook her bones. She grabbed her legs, pinching the flesh of her thighs as stinging feeling slowly came back to her lower appendages. As it did, she took a look around the room: it was still deserted. Outside, she could faintly hear the two men caterwauling as they jibed back and forth, trading crude barbs at each other.

Lena looked all around for a way out, before noticing a sort of partial loft above the room with a ladder leading up to it. At the far end of the loft was a small window. She pulled herself to her unsteady feet and limped to the ladder, grasping it and placing a foot on the lowest rung, when something told her to pause.

She realized the gravediggers had stopped making noise.

Lena stepped back down slowly, listening for any sound at all, searching the shadows of the room not reached by the bare bulb's light.

Finally deciding she was alone, she turned back to the ladder, and found herself face to face with Warden Tolifson.

Lena screamed. Lurching backwards, her foot slipped in the pool of fluids. She went down hard on her rear end. Warden Tolifson moved slowly towards her, taking his time—smiling as he loomed over her. His sibilant voice was barely a whisper that reached her ear.

"Ohhh... someone is in a great deal of trouble, aren't they?" His wide grin seemed to crack his face in two, and revealed jagged, yellowed teeth.

Lena struggled to crawl backwards, away from the approaching vampire. Her mind raced to come up with some kind of escape, but blind panic blocked her thinking.

"What do you expect? For us to just sit there in our cells, waiting for the next time you want a midnight snack?"

"I expect you and the other girls to know your proper place in the order of things—at the bottom."

He reached down and Lena felt his cold hands clutch her by the throat, lifting her up with unearthly strength, until her feet dangled off the ground. She couldn't think. She couldn't breathe.

Tolifson's fangs grew outward as his mouth gaped. "By the way, your little accomplice the Doctor? Well I'm afraid she and her family are going to come to a tragic end tonight."

He leaned in for the kill—when a shovel struck him in the back.

Lena felt herself dropped onto the stony floor. She gasped for air, and looked up in a daze to see the two gravediggers standing off against the enraged Warden, with shovels raised.

"Now you just hold it right there, buddy... no little girls is getting strangled when I'm around, I don't care what they done."

Tolifson sneered at the men: "Now let's don't be foolish, men... you've done your job. Go now and I will forgive your indiscretion."

Muskie shook his head. "You must be hard 'a hearing, bub. Now you gonna stand right there and behave while my cousin gets the sheriff... Doc Mears is a nice lady, ain't nothing bad happening to her and hers tonight."

A glimmer caught Lena's eye, and she began inching backwards ever-so-slowly, so as to not to attract attention.

"Very well," Tolifson hissed. "You're both going to die in the most horrible fashion. As will your own families."

"Well, then. That changes things, don't it, Clifford?

"It does at that, Muskgrove."

The men both lowered their shovels a fraction, and then swung them in unison, battering the Warden over and over again.

"Don't NOBODY threaten our kinfolk, and walks away, mister!" Clifford hollered as he broke his shovel over the Warden's back.

Muskie gave Tolifson a good whack upside the head with his own tool. "Don't worry, partner, we got a good spot for you out back!"

But even as Lena's hand reached out for the glimmering object, Tolifson recovered from his surprise and suddenly erupted upward, ripping the shovel out of Muskie's hand and slashing the steel blade across Clifford's stomach, spilling his guts out. In a moment he'd buried his fangs in Muskie's throat and ripped out his larynx, spitting it on the floor.

As Clifford's body fell, Tolfison spun around, looking for Lena—but saw only the corpse of Hallie on the table.

Lena rose up directly behind the ghoul, raising the scalpel and jabbing it into the back of Tolifson's neck—directly into his spinal column.

The Warden's body convulsed and collapsed to his knees as Lena slowly paced around behind him, crouching a moment to pick up the broken end of Clifford's shovel handle.

With supreme effort Tolifson managed to reach a shaking hand up and yank the scalpel out of his neck. He struggled to stand again, but collapsed back to one knee as the severed nerves of his body betrayed him. His claw-like hands clenched. He opened his mouth and dark blood oozed out of its corner. His voice was now a harsh gurgle.

"You..."

Lena raised the jagged wooden handle. "You know what? I've been waiting for this moment since I first saw you."

With a yell she shoved it home into the center of the Warden's chest. The jagged wood penetrated through wool and flesh and wedged between the bones of his ribs. Warden Tolifson moaned in agony, his eyes rolling up, his arms flailing in futility. Lena stepped in and grabbed hold of the handle

119

once more, shoving it in further. It took her two more pushes before she felt the wood break through the bone and puncture his heart, reaching the spine.

Warden Tolifson collapsed backwards, his nailed fingers scratching at the wood, his features withering and his body shriveling quickly before Lena's eyes, until what was left looked like little more than a centuries-old cadaver.

She stared down at him for a moment to be sure, before turning her gaze to the other three bodies in the room: Hallie on the table, Muskie and Clifford laying on the floor. She whispered quietly to herself:

"No more."

She turned on her heel and left.

20.

LENA RACED THROUGH THE THICK brush of the backwoods, working to keep the tall peaks before her, knowing that way was wWest. The thorny bushes slashed at her exposed thighs and arms, and the rough ground cut at her bare feet, but she kept going for what seemed forever. She gasped in great lungfuls of thick humid air—spitting it back out as she continued for over an hour.

After a while she came to the creek Dr. Mears had told her about. She took a moment as she stepped in, taking relief in the feel of the cool water on her gashes and scrapes. She dipped her hands in and scrubbed the remaining bodily fluids from Hallie away, even taking a moment to take off her dress and soak it before wringing it out, pulling it back on and forging ahead across the water.

Mears had said something about running water. That the Wardens didn't like it. That reminded Lena of something she'd heard, or possibly read, when she was young. If what she'd been told were true, maybe the Wardens wouldn't be able to follow her across the creek. But she wasn't about to bet on it. She clambered up the slippery far bank of the creek and hurried on.

Before long she came to a modest-sized farmhouse sitting by itself on a low rise clear of trees or brush. It had two stories and painted wood siding on the walls, leaded windows, a small portico over the front door, and a driveway with a Hudson sedan parked in it. Inside, the lights were on downstairs, and in one upstairs room.

Lena darted across the grass towards the house, keeping low and hunkered down: watching all around for any signs that the Wardens had beaten her here.

As she came up to the side of the house she flattened herself against it, listening for anything. She peeked into one of the windows, but couldn't see anything through the curtains, so she moved carefully around the outside. She stood up on her tiptoes to look into another window—a living room with furniture, a radio, and kids' toys. No people. Skirting a low hedge, Lena stepped up onto the Mears' front porch, paused a moment to listen, then knocked on the door. She waited, shivering, listening to the sounds around her nervously. After a bit she started to knock again, when a voice halted her hand in midair:

"Hold it right there, woman..."

She turned to see a middle-aged man in a plaid shirt holding a double-barrel shotgun on her.

"You're one of them girls from the prison, ain't you? What you do, escape? Well ain't nothing for you here, lady, you best get moving along..."

Lena chose her words with care: "Please... I need to talk to Dr. Mears... it's more important than you can possibly know."

"Yeah, well that's a shame, but the Doctor ain't feeling well enough to have folk callin' on her tonight." He cocked the hammers on the weapon. "Now this is my property and you ain't got permission to be on't. I don't want to shoot no girl, but I'm within my rights, so you best—"

"You best listen to ME, Mr. Mears. Something's coming for your wife and your children... something from that place. Something I'm sure your wife's only hinted about to you... trust me, it's much worse than you've ever guessed."

His gun lowered an inch.

"What is it?" he asked. His face had gone pale. "What have you brought to my house?"

"Daddy?" a tiny voice broke the tension between the two, and they both turned to look. A small boy was standing in the doorway, watching them through the screen door. He wore an old towel tied around his neck like a cape, and held a wooden sword in one small fist.

"Are the bad men coming?" he asked.

Mears and Lena glanced at one another, then another voice came from inside.

"Yes, Billy. They are."

Doctor Mears stood in the hallway in a shawl, holding onto the handrail for support.

• • •

Lena sat on the Mears' couch, drying herself with a towel. Their son, who'd been introduced to her as Billy, was watching as his parents hurried around, grabbing blankets and canned food and filling up old milk bottles with water. That reminded Lena:

"Doctor, you told me something about running water..."

The Ddoctor nodded, "They don't like to cross running water. It's part of what's kept them contained for so long. That's why we live here, on the other side of the creek."

"But in the truck—I mean we crossed a brook to get to the burial field. And he was in it, so..."

"Something's changed." New worry shadowed Dr. Mears' face. "They know their time is up. They're desperate, and being desperate makes them even more dangerous..."

• • •

A mile away, a shoe stepped tentatively into the trickling water of the creek. The water immediately began to steam at its touch. Warden Skelly grimaced noticeably. He set his jaw and waded into the water, the two Wardens behind him following after.

As they pushed through the creek, it sizzled and hissed around them, burning their flesh causing them unimaginable agony. But then they were across, still smoking from the ordeal. A look between them, and they marched forward.

•   •   •

The hurried packing was done, and Tom Mears nodded to his wife: "Go get Lizzie. We're leaving right now."

As the Doctor hurried upstairs, Billy came over to Lena, dragging his wooden sword. Too young to grasp what was going on, he was aware enough to know they were all in trouble.

Lena nodded to his homemade weapon: "You look like a big tough soldier. You gonna protect your mom and dad?"

He nodded, looking down at the sword.

"You came from the jail where mommy works?"

"Yep."

Billy leaned close: "Are you a crook?"

She smiled just a bit. "Some people think so..."

"You don't look like a crook."

"No?"

He shook his head earnestly. "No, crooks are uuugglllly..."

Staring at the child, Lena was nearly overcome with emotion. She reached out to flatten Billy's shaggy bed hair. It was a simple gesture—one she had done with her own son many, many times. For a moment, Billy disappeared and the specter of Jonathan stood before her, beaming. Happy. Alive.

She shook her head to clear it. Billy yawned sleepily. It was past his bedtime.

"Where are we going, daddy?"

Tom was stacking things by the door to take out to the car: "I'm not sure, Billy. Far away from here, though."

He came over and picked the boy up. Lena stood up to look at himto her, and Lena stood up. There was a moment of mute understanding between them, and she knew what he was going to say before he said it.

"My wife, she's gonna ask you—"

"It's okay. I'm not going with you. They want me too bad. It's too risky."

"I'm sorry. I wish we could. You seem—"

124

"You just take care of your family."

The man put a kind hand on her arm, just for a moment. Then the Doctor was coming back downstairs, holding a sleeping two-year old in her arms.

"I've got Lizzie. Okay, are we ready?"

Tom nodded and picked up the heavy stack of supplies. Lena picked up Billy, and they all headed outside.

Tom stacked all the gear in the backseat, taking the sleepy Billy from Lena. She touched his mop of hair one last time, then started back towards the porch. Doctor Mears looked up at her.

"Well, come on..."

She shook her head. "You folks got a nice place here. I'm gonna stick around a spell."

The Ddoctor took a step towards her: "You can't. They're coming. And they're angry."

"Yeah, but I figure they're more angry at me than you folks right now. That may just buy you a little time. You say they can't stand running water. I hear the Florida Keys are a nice place for a family vacation. Maybe even Cuba?"

Tom was staring at his wife. "Carolyn, we have to—" But then Lena stiffened. She'd seen a subtle, pale shape lurking at the edge of the trees.

"Damn..."

They all turned.

The three Wardens were standing motionless on the lawn, at measured distances from each other in their field, watching them.

"It's too goddamn late."

21.

THERE WAS A HORRIBLE STILL moment as Lena and the Mears family stared at the oncoming shapes. The Doctor's voice was hoarse: "Tom, what do we do?"

"Grab the girl. Back in the house: everyone."

The doctor hesitated, so Lena hurried to the car and took up little Lizzie, leading the way inside.

Behind them, the Wardens slowly advanced.

Inside, Tom Mears locked the door, bracing it with an old two-by-four. Handing little Lizzie to her mother, Lena hurried to close the shutters on all the other windows in the living room.

"This won't stop them, you know."

"What do you suggest?" he asked her. She didn't have an answer. The Doctor was struggling to keep herself together:

"The children... maybe if we beg them they'll spare the—"

Her voice stopped as she caught Lena's look.

"Oh dear God..."

Lena peered out the crack between shutters: "I can only see one of them..."

Mears shook his head. "There were at least four..."

"Five. They're gonna try to come in the back way, too." She thought a moment, and an idea sparked in her mind. "Do you folks have a coal chute?"

"Yeah, but it's narrow. Real narrow."

Lena looked at the kids—at the slender doctor. Tom understood without a word, and grabbed Billy up.

"Where are we going now, daddy?"

"Down to the cellar, son... come on."

Billy reached for his toy sword on the couch: "I need my sword!" But Tom hustled the boy up before he could get it, and they hurried to a door under the stairs. Lena lingered behind. She and Dr. Mears shared one final look, and the Mears family hurried down, closing the cellar door behind them.

The stairs leading down were dark. John picked up a shovel with one hand and wedged it up under the latch of the door, bracing it shut. As he led his family downstairs he grabbed a pickaxe.

"Dadddeee..."

"Hush, son, it's gonna be alright."

Reaching the basement, he put Billy down on his feet, and clambered up a small mound of coal for the furnace, reaching for the hatch to the chute. With some doing, he managed to wrench it open. The opening was indeed very narrow. Maybe eighteen inches across at most. He and his wife shared a look.

Upstairs, Lena was silent and still, listening for to the subtle telltale creaks of the Wardens' steps as they circled the house—watching their uncanny forms cast sharp, angled shadows as they passed by the windows. She knew there was no way for her to make it past them, and even if she did, where would she go? She was miles and miles from any town, a half-naked convicted murderess. Her escape attempt was over. Now her only thought was to hold the creatures off as long as possible, so maybe the Mears' could get away. But even that, she acknowledged, was now unlikely.

She made her way into the kitchen, which was open to the dining and living room. Looking around, she opened the door of the oven, then began pulling open the Mears' drawers—rifling through all their utensils and putting aside the commonplace cutlery. Her search grew more frantic as she suddenly heard scratching from somewhere outside. Finally she spotted a small wooden box on top of the Frigidaire. She reached for it, but still couldn't get hold, so she grabbed a chair from the table and dragged it over.

The chair made a shrill, harsh noise that made her wince, and the creaking movement outside halted for an instant. In a flash Lena stepped up onto the chair and, still having to stretch, grabbed the box and brought it down—just as she heard a resounding crash from the front door being broken down.

Lena jumped down to the floor, dumping the box out to reveal what she was hoping to find: a silver carving knife, the handle reading *Thomas and Carolyn- May 25th, 1926.*

She snatched it up, ducking back into the shadows.

Several Wardens crept like wraiths through the empty living room, their eyes reflecting the room's dim lamplight back. Their flesh was scalded and blistered from the crossing, and their suits now hung in rags.

Warden Evers paused, catching something out of the corner of his eye, and moved forward to investigate.

Down in the cellar the family stared up as they heard the soft creaks of the Warden's footsteps, seeing the gentle rain of dust from the floorboards above. After a moment, Tom went back to lifting his children up to the coal chute.

"Go on, now, climb up..."

"Why, Daddy? Is it like a game?"

The Ddoctor whispered: "Yes, honey. It's like a game. Now be quiet as you can..." Together they watched them climb.

"Tom."

"Go on, you can fit. Here—" He helped her up, sending a tiny avalanche of coal rolling down off the pile.

Above, Warden Evers had his ear to the cellar door, listening patiently. Finally he was rewarded as he caught the sound of a few metallic bumps, as Doctor Mears tried to clamber up the chute. His face cracked into a sinister smile as he reached for the doorknob, but turned to a frown as it didn't budge. He gripped it harder. The door held.

Meanwhile, Lena waited in the shadows.

Growing impatient, Warden Evers brought his arm back and smashed his fist through the basement door, reaching through and wrenching the shovel handle out of the way. He jerked the door open to see Tom standing waiting for him at the bottom of the stairs, holding the pickaxe.

"Found you!" the creature crackled.

Only a dozen feet away, Tarker, Oberlun and Kleig were making their way into the kitchen, then Warden Tarker stopped them with an upraised hand:

He could see the oven was open and unlit. The toaster on the counter was on and smoking, with handles of silverware sticking out.

Tarker screamed "OUT!" and they all turned, but it was too late.

Immediately below the kitchen window, Doctor Mears was struggling to worm her way out of the coal chute, Billy helping her by tugging on her collar, when a huge burst of flame exploded out of the kitchen window above their heads.

Thrown by the concussion of the blast, Warden Evers tumbled down the stairs. He landed flat on his back, momentarily dazed. As he shook his head to clear it, he realized Tom Mears was standing above him with the pickaxe.

"Sorry... but I believe you're trespassing."

He raised the axe up and brought it down again. It sank into Warden Evers' heart, going through to glace off the brick floor in a shower of sparks. Evers shrieked an unearthly animal howl, clawing at the air with raking nails as Tom stumbled back. Slowly the vampire's thrashing subsided, as his body rapidly decayed, reduced to an emaciated husk within seconds.

Black acrid smoke from the blast was billowing out of the kitchen. Warden Oberlun took a few stumbling steps into the living room—his flesh burned to a crisp—and fell face down. Warden Kleig, only partially burned but blinded from the fireball, emerged after him. He grabbed the wall for support, stumbling to one knee. That was when Lena emerged from the dark pantry behind him.

Even blind, Kleig's paranormal senses told him where she was and he spun, grabbing her by the throat and lifting her off the floorboards.

"You have caused an inordinate amount of damage, little girl... your death will be agonizing in a way you can scarcely comprehend! I will personally—" He was cut off as she slashed out with her silver knife, cutting cleanly through his throat. What seemed like ten gallons of dark, bile-like blood erupted out of the gash, covering Lena.

Kleig sagged to his knees clutching at his throat, his rotten blood still gushing out all over the wooden floor. Lena stepped slowly around the wounded creature struggling to hold his lifeblood in with his hand, grasping his scalp and pulling his head harshly back, the blade to his mangled gullet.

"It was you, wasn't it? The one who took my son?"

Warden Kleig shook his head. His voice is a barely-audible gurgle through half-severed vocal cords.

"No... not me... Our master's privilege... Skellllyyy...."

His eyes rolled up. With cold dispassion, Lena sliced away at the bone and sinewy connecting tissue still holding Kleig's head to his torso, before it finally came off and fell into the pool of rank blood at her feet. Both body parts quickly began smoking, and then all that was left were skeletal ashes.

Lena stared at them for some few moments until a voice startled her:.

"Jeez, that's a lotta blood."

She turned to see Tom Mears behind her.

"Yeah, well he's had a lot of years to store it up."

He was counting the bodies lying all around: "There's one still left." He began to step forward, but Lena held up a hand.

"No. Get your family. This one is mine."

He started to go. "You gonna be—?"

"I'll be fine. Thanks. And Tom?"

"Yeah?"

"Real sorry about your kitchen."

He almost smiled. "Yeah."

As Tom Mears headed out the back door, Lena starting moving towards the smoky living room, and as she did, she began singing softly to herself:

"Far from home, burned and alone..."

22.

LENA CROSSED INTO THE LIVING room, picking up random family ornaments: a baseball mitt, a ball of yarn, one of Lizzie's dolls. When she reached the center, she stopped, sensing the presence of another.

"I knew you'd come last. That's your privilege, isn't it?"

Warden Skelly seemed to materialize before her out of the smoke and shadow.

"What can you hope to know of our ways, child? We have been what we are since before your wretched species could draw crude pictures on cave walls."

Lena smirked at the fiend: "Not a lot to show for all that time... just ghouls lurking in the dark, preying on helpless girls..."

They began to slowly circle each other.

"Ah, yes... you creatures are so proud of your puny accomplishments... you've managed to cover half the planet with your spawn... built factories that spew filth into the air, flown cumbersome hunks of metal across the oceans... all because you can walk in the Sun. But for that, your kind would still all be living in pens, for us to eat as we please, as it should have been."

"That's why the prison... a reminder of better times, huh?"

His eyes glittered.

"Simpler times."

She braced herself: "And my son?"

"Simply a method to acquire you, my dear. Your name was... provided to us by your boss—swarthy little man, if I recall."

"Lonnie. That bastard..."

Skelly's tone grew reflective: "There was a time when we could take whomever we chose... but crime and lawlessness have dwindled in this age, and lately we've have to—recruit—new guests. Lowly wretches, with nobody to miss them. People with nothing to live for."

Lena stopped pacing. "You're wrong. I had HIM to live for. He was all I had. And you took him."

"And you have now taken several of my kin. Are we not now equal?"

"You and I will *never* be equals."

He digested that a moment.

"I'm going to end your life very soon, now... But I'm wondering how I misjudged you so badly? You were a meek little creature, not even a real killer like the others..."

Lena's mouth cracked at the corners: "Is that what you thought?"

Skelly paused a moment, then he understood.

"Your missing husband..."

"Was a drunk. And a bully... but he was insured."

The vampire gave a little cackle, a sound like dead leaves blowing across a stone. Lena's eyes searched the room for anything to use against him, and found something.

"How nice. Two killers in a room. Like the beginning of some old joke."

"I don't think you're gonna find the punchline to this one very funny."

"You are going to die, now, Miss Cole."

She tensed: "Fine. I'm ready."

He came leaping at her with blinding speed. But Lena was prepared. Even as he was in midair she reached around and snatched up Billy's wooden sword. As Skelly fell upon her, grabbing her and taking her to the floor, his jaws chomping down on her throat, he impaled himself upon it.

They hit the floor as one, skidding across the wood, knocking over the dining room table and chairs.

Skelly's face reared back, contorted in agony, fangs bared—dripping Lena's own blood onto her face.

Lena set her jaw and shoved the sword in deeper, until its bloody tip burst out of the vampire's back. Skelly thrashed like an animal on top of her, his claws digging large furrows in the wooden floor. Lena dodged her head right and left as his teeth gnashed at her neck.

She could feel his body sagging against her as he went through his final death throes. Without all the blood, he seemed to become much lighter, and Lena was finally able to get her feet under his stomach and shove him off her with a mighty kick, sending him flipping over backwards.

Warden Skelly slammed down onto his back, the toy sword still protruding from his chest. Even as his skin began to flake and fall away from his bones, his spasmatic, taloned hands struggled to remove it.

But Lena was back on top of him in an instant, straddling him, putting all her weight onto the toy and keeping it in place, even as he clawed at her skin—raking red marks across her cheeks.

The Head Warden of Steelgate Prison choked a few final, unintelligible syllables, as Lena stared down at him with rapt intensity.

"Die!" she screamed at him, and again:

"DIE!"

And, finally, he did. The last air went out of him like a burst balloon, and his body crumpled under her, leaving her straddling a shriveled skeleton.

Lena stared down at what remained of her son's killer. She had forced down the grief and agony for so long now, so many months, that she had almost forgotten their intensity. Those feelings came rushing back over her like a tidal swell, and her tears finally came, falling to sizzle on the killer's desiccated bones.

Finally a gentle hand touched her shoulder.

Lena looked up to see Doctor Mears, her husband, and children standing behind her. Gently but firmly, Tom lifted Lena up and away from the pile of cinders that for so many centuries, possibly even millennia, had been Warden Skelly.

But no more.

•　　•　　•

As they drove away in the Mears' Hudson, Lena sat curled up under a blanket in the back seat. Billy's head lay in her lap as he slept, and she gently brushed his hair. Her life, she now came to realize, had always been a study of duality. Like a seesaw, rocking back and forth between complete joy and abject desperation. She had lost more than she would have thought she could live through... and yet, she lived.

23.

1934

THE GENTLE WAVES ROLLED UP over the sandy beach and around Lena's bare ankles in a gentle caress unlike anything she'd ever felt in her previous life. This was her favorite time of day here on the island. As the sun lowered over the water, there was a certain way its light suffused the air, making the whole world seem to glow with a muted, comfortable radiance.

She stood staring at the water for an unknown time—time itself was less important here. The days and nights blended together, but in a different way than they had in that hellish prison: there the monotony of her environment had worn down the mind, eliminating the innumerable, wonderful little differences each day on earth held.

Here, instead, those differences became little benchmarks, blending into a wondrous flow of days and nights and nights and days. On Sunday she had walked up the coast further than ever before, taking with her a small cheesecloth wrapped sandwich to eat. Tuesday there had been a heavy rain that had spent itself quickly, leaving a crackling clarity to the air all around. Wednesday she'd made bread with Dr. Mears in the small clay oven behind their house, and today she'd spent some time staring at the horizon—and past it towards the invisible shore of the country they'd left behind, with its horrors and losses—reflecting on this new life and place she'd found for herself, thanks to the kindness of the Mears family.

The linen dress wrapped around her covered many of her scars, but several still stood out white against her browned skin, slashing down her face and neck. She didn't mind them. They were the only physical proof of what she had gone through, and she was happy they'd stay with her for the rest of her life.

The lower curve of the sun was now almost touching the distant horizon, lighting the tips of millions of tiny sea swells with ochre fire. As she stood staring, Lena felt a gentle touch to her hand and looked down to find Billy standing next to her. In the year since they'd first met at the Mears house that cataclysmic night, he'd grown a full three inches, and as she put her arm around him and hugged him to her side, the idea passed through her mind like a swift bird that for every thing life had taken from her, it had given something back.

"Dad says it's almost time to eat, Aunt Lena." His tanned face glowed in the ephemeral light.

"Well we shouldn't keep them waiting, should we?"

Together they turned to trek up the sand to the small cottage standing at the trees' edge, stopping on the way to collect young Lizzie—now a meandering toddler.

Lena had suffered through things that normal people could not fathom, and yet those tortures had not destroyed her. She could still find joy in the world around her; in little, simple things like the feel of the sun on her face, the sound of ocean waves, and the laughter of small voices.

It began to drizzle, and the three broke into a clumsy, laughing dash towards where Tom and Carolyn were waiting for them.

ABOUT THE AUTHOR

JIM TOWNS IS A WRITER, director and visual artist. His films include the silent expressionist feature *Prometheus Triumphant: a Fugue in the Key of Flesh*, the award-winning haunted heist film *House of Bad*, the post-apocalyptic drama *State of Desolation*, and the streaming series *Immortal Hands*.

His short fiction has been published in print and online by *Burial Day*, *Switchblade Magazine*, *Pulp Modern*, *Castle of Horror*, and many more. He is the author of the non-fiction book *American Cryptic*, and *Whiskey Stories*, a collection of his poems, writings and photographs, will be released in 2022 by Uncle B Publications.

His paintings and mixed media artwork have been exhibited in galleries in Pittsburgh, New York and Los Angeles.

He currently lives in San Pedro, CA with his wife and several mysterious cats.

If you liked *Bloodsucker City*, you might also enjoy reading the following titles available on Amazon from Castle Bridge Media:

Austinites By In Churl Yo

THE CASTLE OF HORROR ANTHOLOGY SERIES
Castle Of Horror Anthology Volume 1
Castle of Horror Anthology Volume 2: Holiday Horrors
Castle of Horror Anthology Volume 3: Scary Summer Stories
Castle of Horror Anthology Volume 4: Women Running From Houses
Castle of Horror Anthology Volume 5: Thinly Veiled: The 70s
Castle of Horror Anthology Volume 6: Femme Fatales
Edited By Jason Henderson (Vol. 6 Edited by P.J. Hoover)

Castle of Horror Podcast Book of Great Horror:
Our Favorites, Top Tens, and Bizarre Pleasures
Edited By Jason Henderson

FuturePast Sci-Fi Anthology
Edited by In Churl Yo

Isonation By In Churl Yo

THE PATH
Book 1: The Blue-Spangled Blue By David Bowles
Book 2: The Deepest Green By David Bowles

Surf Mystic: Night of the Book Man By Peyton Douglas

Nightwalkers: Gothic Horror Movies By Bruce Lanier Wright

Please remember to leave us your reviews on Amazon and Goodreads!

CASTLE BRIDGE MEDIA
DENVER, COLORADO, USA

THANK YOU FOR SUPPORTING INDEPENDENT PUBLISHERS AND AUTHORS!

castlebridgemedia.com

www.ingramcontent.com/pod-product-compliance
Lightning Source LLC
Chambersburg PA
CBHW052005220626
47052CB00004B/1104